The Blood of the Conquerors

The Gregg Press Western Fiction Series
Priscilla Oaks, Editor

The Blood of the Conquerors

Harvey Fergusson

with a new introduction by
William T. Pilkington

Gregg Press

A division of G. K. Hall & Co., Boston, 1978

This is a complete photographic reprint of a work first published in New York by Alfred A. Knopf in 1921.

Text copyright 1921 by Alfred A. Knopf, Inc.
Reprinted by arrangement with Francis Fergusson.
Introduction copyright © 1978 by William T. Pilkington.

Grateful acknowledgment is made to Saul Cohen for generously providing a rare early copy of *The Blood of the Conquerors* for reproduction in this Gregg Press edition.

Frontmatter designed by Designworks, Inc. of Cambridge, Massachusetts.

Printed on permanent/durable acid-free paper and bound in the United States of America.

Republished in 1978 by Gregg Press, A Division of G. K. Hall & Co., 70 Lincoln Street, Boston, Massachusetts 02111.

First Printing, October 1978

Library of Congress Cataloging in Publication Data

Fergusson, Harvey, 1890–1971.
  The blood of the conquerors.

  (The Gregg Press western fiction series)
  Reprint of the ed. published by Knopf,
New York.
  I. Title. II. Series.
[PZ3.F388Bl 1978] [PS3511.E55] 813'.5'2
ISBN 0-8398-2470-X 78-13369

Introduction

The Blood of the Conquerors, published in 1921, was the first of Harvey Fergusson's 14 books (ten of which were novels). Fergusson, who was born in Albuquerque, New Mexico in 1890, began his writing career as a newspaper reporter. For about a decade, beginning in 1912, he worked for a number of East Coast and Middlewestern newspapers, though during most of that time he was stationed in Washington, D. C. In the course of his reportorial duties he interviewed and wrote an admiring story about H. L. Mencken. The two immediately became close acquaintances, with the older man, Mencken, taking a fatherly and solicitous interest in the young newspaperman's career. Mencken wisely encouraged Fergusson to try his hand at kinds of writing more serious and less ephemeral than journalism.

In 1919 Fergusson began finally to put down on paper a tale of the contemporary Southwest—"contemporary," of course, at the time of composition—that had evolved in his imagination over a period of several years. Working mainly on weekends and during vacations, he completed a manuscript by early 1921. He took the story to Mencken, who was on the board of directors of the Alfred A. Knopf publishing company, and Mencken saw to it that the manuscript was published, under the title *The Blood of the Conquerors*, and that the book's dust jacket was adorned with enthusiastic blurbs. For much of the decade of the 1920s, Fergusson, working under Mencken's tutelage, was regarded as an extremely promising young author who might some day become a major American literary figure.

Yet in the ensuing years Fergusson's writing career never seemed to fulfill the promise of its beginnings. Though he continued to turn out serious fiction and nonfiction, the writer found it necessary to support himself primarily by grinding out frivolous stories for the mass-circulation periodicals and by working as a screenwriter for various Hollywood motion picture companies. By the 1930s critics and reviewers had begun to dismiss him as a minor regional fictionist, since most of his novels to that point were laid in the American West. But even in the West, Fergusson never managed during his lifetime to acquire the recognition that his works clearly merit. Other recent Western writers—Walter Van Tilburg Clark, Vardis Fisher, A. B. Guthrie, Wallace Stegner, Frederick Manfred—have reputations as serious regional artists that seem to outweigh Fergusson's modest renown. I do not hesitate to claim, however, that Fergusson's achievement is easily the equal of that of his more celebrated colleagues. The best of the author's novels—*The Blood of the Conquerors, Wolf Song* (1927), *In Those Days* (1929), *Grant of Kingdom* (1950), and *The Conquest of Don Pedro* (1954) —comprise as distinguished a body of fiction as any yet fashioned by a writer from the American West.

When he died in Berkeley, California in 1971, Fergusson had lived to enjoy at least a modicum of long-delayed recognition and acclaim. During the last couple of decades of his life, several writers and collectors of Western literature "discovered" his books and attempted to call more general attention to them. Saul Cohen, Lawrence Clark Powell, and John R. Milton deserve special mention for their pioneering efforts in this regard. Critics have begun in recent years to examine the works in detail in order to isolate their special virtues. Cecil Robinson, for instance, in his highly regarded *With the Ears of Strangers: The Mexican in American Literature* (Tucson: University of Arizona Press, 1963), comments lengthily and admiringly on a half-dozen of Fergusson's best regional books. James K. Folsom's pamphlet, *Harvey Fergusson* (Austin, Texas: Steck-Vaughn, 1969), supplies a useful introductory essay on the writer's philosophy and fictional concerns. William T. Pilkington's *Harvey Fergusson* (Boston: Twayne Publishers, 1975) is the first book-length biographical-critical study of the author, and includes full analyses of each of the works. As favorable critical responses accumulate, acknowledgement of Fergusson's accomplishment grows. Hopefully the writer's posthumous reputation will acquire, in the not-too-distant future, dimensions more commensurate with his actual, very considerable achievement.

The Blood of the Conquerors is not at the pinnacle of Fergusson's very best fiction. It is nevertheless a surprisingly good and still relevant book, certainly one that ought to be made available to a new generation of readers. Apparently the story sprang from both personal and generalized experiences in the author's early life. Fergusson's sister Erna—in her book *Our Southwest* (New York: Alfred A. Knopf, Inc., 1940)—suggests that the novel's central character, Ramon Delcasar, was modeled after a real person, "a playmate, a schoolmate with whom he vied for his first girl." On a more generalized level, *The Blood of the Conquerors* chronicles a social phenomenon—the decline of New Mexico's Spanish aristocracy—that reached its completion during the years Fergusson was growing up in Albuquerque. Cecil Robinson, in *With the Ears of Strangers*, judges the novel to be an authentic historical portrait of "the old Mexican families of the Albuquerque region in full decay and in the final stages of what was to become an almost total dispossession." The pathetic denouement of that dispossession Fergusson witnessed at first hand; his observations form the social backdrop of *The Blood of the Conquerors*.

The Spanish settlers, who first came to what is now New Mexico in the seventeenth century, brought with them an already outmoded feudal social structure. This structure was ruled by a small, privileged aristocratic class—the *ricos* ("rich ones")—at the top and supported at its base by the much larger class of *peones*, who were as closely tied to the land and to their aristocratic masters as were the medieval serfs. Life in such an enclosed, isolated society was pastoral and easygoing, attuned to a relaxed tempo that seemed an unchanging quality of that unique way of life. The fatal disruption of this two-centuries-old social structure began with the arrival, in the middle decades of the 19th century, of the Anglos, who carried with them a new, money-oriented social ethic and an entirely different concept of time and work. By means of violence, trickery, and in many cases simply greater energy and ambition, the Anglos inexorably appropriated the *nativos'* land, wealth, and political power. As portrayed in *The Blood of the Conquerors*—which is set in 1912 in a town that is not named, but is obviously Albuquerque—the effects of these changing conditions were reflected most dramatically in the altered fortunes of the old *rico* families, such as the Delcasars. The effects on the *peones*, who found adjustment to a new social system as baffling and difficult as did their *patrons*, were in some ways just as disastrous; the fate of the *peones* was, however, more ambiguous and perhaps did not seem to Fergusson as exciting material for fiction as did the more clearcut decline of the *ricos*.

Ramon Delcasar, the protagonist of *The Blood of the Conquerors*, attempts to play the Anglos' game. He goes to law school, where he masters the principles of the Anglo legal system. He wins, for a time, the affections of a cultured Eastern girl whom (as he admits to himself late in the novel) he loves more for what she represents—the shiny surface attractions of the Anglo world—than for what she really is. He amasses land and money, and shows himself adept at acquiring political power in the new "democratic" system. And yet, by Anglo standards, he fails miserably. At story's end he has given up, having retired with his common-law wife to a small farm near his native town. His house is a crumbling hacienda, once the seat of a powerful *rico* family. This last detail seems to suggest that Ramon has retreated into the past, where he dreams of the glories of yesteryear as he wastes away in the greatly reduced circumstances of a static present.

What accounts for the acute arc of Ramon's spectacular rise and fall? Fergusson's answer to that question appears to be that Ramon is a "primitive" man who, finally, suffers the consequences of his anachronistic heritage and discovers that he cannot adapt to a modern society. Time and again in the novel, Fergusson makes comments such as the following: "He had the love of sensuous indolence which, together with its usual complement, the capacity for brief but violent action, marked him as a primitive man—one whom the regular labors and restraints of civilization would never fit" (p. 248).

The author's assumption of an irreconcilable conflict between "primitive" and "civilized" approaches to life is one that not all readers will share. But most will agree, I think, that cultural conditioning is a strong determinant of behavior. Certainly the "clash of cultures" is a recurrent theme in ethnic literature, because cultural conflict does often have dire effects on people's lives. Ramon is suspended between two worlds, two cultures. He hovers there for a time, then is cruelly tossed aside and left a moldering, apathetic victim of his society's divisions and of his own ambivalent impulses. Ramon's is an old story, but a timely one, for such scenarios are lived out today, even as they were in 1912.

As I mentioned earlier, I do not rank *The Blood of the Conquerors* as one of Fergusson's very best fictions. Problems of plot structure and of implausible characterization damage the book's overall effectiveness. Perhaps most distracting of all is the presence throughout the work of a strong authorial voice that is often obtrusive, sometimes to the point of temporarily damming up the narrative flow. These are weaknesses that may be chalked up to inexperience; the book was, we must remember, a first novel. Though flawed, *The Blood of the Conquerors* is nonetheless a highly readable and illuminating regional novel. One of the book's more remarkable features is its continuing relevance to a rapidly changing world. More than half a century after its first publication, *The Blood of the Conquerors* remains a suggestive fictional study of problems—the clash of cultures and of ethnic groups, and the prejudice and misunderstanding that issue from that clash—which still torment the West and Southwest, and indeed the nation as a whole.

William T. Pilkington
Tarleton State University
Stephenville, Texas

*The Blood of
the Conquerors*

CHAPTER I

Whenever Ramon Delcasar boarded a railroad train he indulged a habit, not uncommon among men, of choosing from the women passengers the one whose appearance most pleased him to be the object of his attention during the journey. If the woman were reserved or well-chaperoned, or if she obviously belonged to another man, this attention might amount to no more than an occasional discreet glance in her direction. He never tried to make her acquaintance unless her eyes and mouth unmistakably invited him to do so.

This conservatism on his part was not due to an innate lack of self-confidence. Whenever he felt sure of his social footing, his attitude toward women was bold and assured. But his social footing was a peculiarly uncertain thing for the reason that he was a Mexican. This meant that he faced in every social contact the possibility of a more or less covert prejudice against his blood, and that he faced it with an unduly proud and sensitive spirit concealed beneath a manner of aristocratic indifference. In the little southwestern town where he had lived all his life, except the last three years, his social position was ostensibly of the highest. He was spoken of as belonging to an old and prominent family. Yet he knew of mothers who carefully guarded their daughters from the peril of falling in love with him, and most of his boyhood fights had started when some one called him a "damned Mexican" or a "greaser."

Except to an experienced eye there was little in his appearance or in his manner to suggest his race. His swarthy complexion indicated perhaps a touch of the Moorish blood in his Spanish ancestry, but he was no darker than are many Americans bearing Anglo-Saxon names, and his eyes were grey. His features were aquiline and pleasing, and he had in a high degree that bearing, at once proud and unself-conscious, which is called aristocratic. He spoke English with a very slight Spanish accent.

When he had gone away to a Catholic law school in St. Louis, confident of his speech and manner and appearance, he had believed that he was leaving prejudice behind him; but in this he had been disappointed. The raw spots in his consciousness, if a little less irritated at the college, were by no means healed. Some persons, it is true, seemed to think nothing of his race one way or the other; to some, mostly women, it gave him an added interest; but in the long run it worked against him. It kept him out of a fraternity, and it made his career in football slow and hard.

When he finally won the coveted position of quarterback, in spite of team politics, he made a reputation by the merciless fashion in which he drove his eleven, and by the fury of his own playing.

The same bitter emulative spirit which had impelled him in football drove him to success in his study of the law. Books held no appeal for him, and he had no definite ambitions, but he had a good head and a great desire to show the gringos what he could do. So he had graduated high in his class, thrown his diploma into the bottom of his trunk, and departed from his alma mater without regret.

The limited train upon which he took passage for home afforded specially good opportunity for his habit of mental philandering. The passengers were continually going up and down between the dining car at one end of the train and the observation car at the other, so that all of the women daily passed in review. They were an unusually attractive lot, for most of the passengers were wealthy easterners on their way to California. Ramon had never before seen together so many women of the kind that devotes time and money and good taste to the business of creating charm. Perfectly gowned and groomed, delicately scented, they filled him with desire and with envy for the men who owned them. There were two newly married couples among the passengers, and several intense flirtations were under way before the train reached Kansas City. Ramon felt as though he were a spectator at some delightful carnival. He was lonely and restless, yet fascinated.

For no opportunity of becoming other than a spectator had come to him. He had chosen without difficulty the girl whom he preferred, but had only dared to admire her from afar. She was a little blonde person, not more than twenty, with angelic grey eyes, hair of the colour of ripe wheat and a complexion of perfect pink and white. The number of different costumes which she managed to don in two days filled him with amazement and gave her person an ever-varying charm and interest. She appeared always accompanied by a very placid-looking and portly woman, who was evidently her mother, and a tall, cadaverous sick man, whose indifferent and pettish attitude toward her seemed to indicate that he was either a brother or an uncle, for Ramon felt sure that she was not married. She acquired no male attendants, but sat most of the time very properly, if a little restlessly, with her two companions. Once or twice Ramon felt her look upon him, but she always turned it away when he glanced at her.

Whether because she was really beautiful in her own petite way, or because she seemed so unattainable, or because her small blonde daintiness had a peculiar appeal for him, Ramon soon reached a state of conviction that she interested him more than any other girl he had ever seen. He discreetly followed her about the train, watching for the opportunity that never came, and consoling himself with the fact that no one else seemed more fortunate in winning her favour than he. The only strange male who attained to the privilege of addressing her was a long-winded and elderly gentleman of the British perpetual-travelling type, at least one representative of which is found on every transcontinental train, and it was plain enough that he bored the girl.

Ramon took no interest in landscapes generally, but when he awoke on the last morning of his journey and found himself once more in the wide and desolate country of his birth, he was so deeply stirred and interested that he forgot all about the girl. Devotion to one particular bit of soil is a Mexican characteristic, and in Ramon it was highly developed because he had spent so much of his life close to the earth. Every summer of his boyhood he had been sent to one of the sheep ranches which belonged to the various branches of his numerous family. Each of these ranches was merely a headquarters where the sheep were annually dipped and sheared and from which the herds set out on their long wanderings across the open range. Often Ramon had followed them—across the deserts where the heat shimmered and the yellow dust hung like a great pale plume over the rippling backs of the herd, and up to the summer range in the mountains where they fed above the clouds in lush green pastures crowned with spires of rock and snow. He had shared the beans and mutton and black coffee of the herders and had gone to sleep on a pile of peltries to the evensong of the coyotes that hung on the flanks of the herd. Hunting, fishing, wandering, he had lived like a savage and found the life good.

It was this life of primitive freedom that he had longed for in his exile. He had thought little of his family and less of his native town, but a nostalgia for open spaces and free wanderings had been always with him. He had come to hate the city with its hard walled-in ways and its dirty air, and also the eastern country-side with its little green prettiness surrounded by fences. He longed for a land where one can see for fifty miles, and not a man or a house. He thought that alkaline dust on his lips would taste sweet.

Now he saw again the scorched tawny levels, the red hills dotted with little gnarled *pinon* trees, the purple mystery of distant mountains. A great friendly warmth filled his body, and his breath came a little quickly with eagerness. When he saw a group of Mexicans jogging along the road on their scrawny mounts he wanted to call out to them: *"Como lo va, amigos?"* He would have liked to salute this whole country, which was his country, and to tell it how glad he was to see it again. It was the one thing in the world that he loved, and the only thing that had ever given him pleasure without tincture of bitterness.

He heard two men in the seat behind him talking.

"Did you ever see anything so desolate?" one asked.

" I wouldn't live in this country if they gave it to me," said the other.

Ramon turned and looked at them. They were solid, important-looking men, and having visited upon the country their impressive disapproval, they opened newspapers and shut it away from their sight. Dull fools, thought Ramon, who do not know God's country when they see it.

And then he continued to look right over their heads and their newspapers, for tripping down the aisle all by herself at last, came the girl of his fruitless choice. His eyes, deep with dreams, met hers. She smiled upon him, radiantly, blushed a little, and hurried on through the car.

He sat looking after her with a foolish grin on his face. He was pleased and shaken. So she

CHAPTER II

Usually in each generation of a large and long-established family there is some one individual who stands out from the rest as a leader and as the most perfect embodiment of the family traditions and characteristics. This was especially true of the Delcasar family. It was established in this country in the year 1790 by Don Eusabio Maria Delcasar y Morales, an officer in the army of the King of Spain, who distinguished himself in the conquest of New Mexico, and especially in certain campaigns against the Navajos. As was customary at that time, the King rewarded his faithful soldier with a grant of land in the new province. This Delcasar estate lay in the Rio Grande Valley and the surrounding *mesa* lands. By the provisions of the King's grant, its dimensions were each the distance that Don Delcasar could ride in a day. The Don chose good horses and did not spare them, so that he secured to his family more than a thousand square miles of land with a strip of rich valley through the middle and a wilderness of desert and mountain on either side. Much of this principality was never seen by Don Eusabio, and even the four sons who divided the estate upon his death had each more land than he could well use.

The outstanding figure of this second generation was Don Solomon Delcasar, who was noted for the magnificence of his establishment, and for his autocratic spirit.

No Borgia or Bourbon ever ruled more absolutely over his own domain than did Don Solomon over the hundreds of square miles which made up his estate. He owned not only lands and herds but also men and women. The *peones* who worked his lands were his possessions as much as were his horses. He had them beaten when they offended him and their daughters were his for the taking. He could not sell them, but this restriction did not apply to the Navajo and Apache slaves whom he captured in war. These were his to be sold or retained for his own use as he preferred. Adult Indians were seldom taken prisoner, as they were untamable, but boys and girls below the age of fifteen were always taken alive, when possible, and were valued at five hundred *pesos* each. Don Solomon usually sold the boys, as he had plenty of *peones*, but he never sold a comely Indian girl.

The Don was a man of proud and irascible temper, but kindly when not crossed. He had been known to kill a *peon* in a fit of anger, and then afterward to bestow all sorts of benefits upon the man's wife and children.

The life of his home, like that of all the other Mexican gentlemen in his time, was an easy and pleasant one. He owned a great *adobe* house, built about a square courtyard like a fort, and shaded pleasantly by cottonwood trees. There he dwelt with his numerous family, his *peones* and his slaves. In the spring and summer every one worked in the fields, though not too hard. In the fall the men went east to the great plains to kill a supply of buffalo meat for the winter, and often after the hunt they travelled south into Sonora and Chihuahua to trade mustangs and buffalo hides for woven goods and luxuries.

There was a pleasant social life among the aristocrats of dances and visits. Marriages, funerals and christenings were occasions of great ceremony and social importance. Indeed everything done by the Dons was characterized by much formality and ceremony, the custom of which had been brought over from Spain. But they were no longer really in touch with Spanish civilization. They never went back to the mother country. They had no books save the Bible and a few other religious works, and many of them never learned to read these. Their lives were made up of fighting, with the Indians and also among themselves, for there were many feuds; of hunting and primitive trade; and of venery upon a generous and patriarchal scale. They were Spanish gentlemen by descent, all for honour and tradition and sentiment; but by circumstance they were barbarian lords, and their lives were full of lust and blood.

Circumstance somewhat modified the vaunted purity of their Spanish blood, too. The Indian slave girls who lived in their houses bore the children of their sons, and some of these half-bred and quarter-bred children were eventually accepted by the *gente de razon*, as the aristocrats called themselves. In this way a strain of Navajo blood got into the Delcasar family, and doubtless did much good, as all of the Spanish stock was weakened by much marrying of cousins.

Dona Ameliana Delcasar, a sister of Don Solomon, was responsible for another alien infusion which ultimately percolated all through the family, and has been thought by some to be responsible for the unusual mental ability of certain Delcasars. Dona Ameliana, a beautiful but somewhat unruly girl, went into a convent in Durango, Mexico, at the age of fifteen. At the age of eighteen she eloped with a French priest named Raubien, who was a man of unusual intellect and a poet. The errant couple came to New Mexico and took up lands. They were excommunicated, of course, and both of them were buried in unconsecrated ground; but despite their spiritual handicaps they raised a family of eleven comely daughters, all of whom married well, several of them into the Delcasar family. Thus some of the Delcasars who boasted of their pure Castilian blood were really of a mongrel breed, comprising along with the many strains that have mingled in Spain, those of Navajo and French.

Don Solomon Delcasar played a brilliant part in the military activities which marked the winning of Mexican Independence from Spain in the eighteen-twenties, and also in the incessant Indian wars. He was a fighter by necessity, but also by choice. They shed blood with grace and nonchalance in those days, and the Delcasars were always known as dangerous men.

The most curious thing about this régime of the old-time Dons was the way in which it persisted. It received its first serious blow in 1845 when the military forces of the United States took possession of New Mexico. Don Jesus Christo Delcasar, who was then the richest and most powerful of the family, was suspected of being a party to the conspiracy which brought about the Taos massacre—the last organized resistance made to the gringo domination. At this time some of the Delcasars went to Old Mexico to live, as did a good many others among the Dons, feeling that the old ways of life in New Mexico were sure to change, and having the Spanish aversion to any departure from tradition. But their fears were not realized, and life went on as before. In 1865 the *peones* and Indian slaves were formally set free, but all of them immediately went deeply in debt to their former masters and thus retained in effect the same status as before. So it happened that in the seventies, when New York was growing into a metropolis, and the factory system was fastening itself upon New England, and the middle west was getting fat and populous and tame, life in the Southwest remained much as it had been a century before.

Laws and governments were powerless there to change ways of life, as they have always been, but two parallel bars of steel reaching across the prairies brought change with them, and it was great and sudden. The railroad reached the Rio Grande Valley early in the eighties, and it smashed the colourful barbaric pattern of the old life as the ruthless fist of an infidel might smash a stained glass window. The metropolis of the northern valley in those days was a sleepy little *adobe* town of a few hundred people, reclining about its dusty *plaza* near the river. The railroad, scorning to notice it, passed a mile away. Forthwith a new town began growing up between the old one and the railroad. And this new town was such a town as had never before been seen in all the Southwest. It was built of wood and only half painted. It was ugly, noisy and raw. It was populated largely by real estate agents, lawyers, politicians and bar-keepers. It cared little for joy, leisure, beauty or tradition. Its God was money and its occupation was business.

This thing called business was utterly strange to the Delcasars and to all of the other Dons. They were men of the saddle, fighting men, and traders only in a primitive way. Business seemed to them a conspiracy to take their lands and their goods away from them, and a remarkably success-ful conspiracy. Debt and mortgage and specula-tion were the names of its weapons. Some of the Dons, including many of the Delcasars, who were now a very numerous family, owning each a com-fortable homestead but no more, sold out and went to Old Mexico. Many who stayed lost all they had in a few years, and degenerated into petty politicians or small storekeepers. Some clung to a bit of land and went on farming, making always less and less money, sinking into poverty and insig-nificance, until some of them were no better off than the men who had once been their *peones*.

Diego Delcasar and Felipe Delcasar, brothers, were two who owned houses in the Old Town and farms nearby, who stayed in the country and held their own for a time and after a fashion. Diego

[21]

Delcasar was far the more able of the two, and a true scion of his family. He caught onto the gringo methods to a certain extent. He divided some farm land on the edge of town into lots and sold them for a good price. With the money he bought a great area of mountain land in the northern part of the state, where he raised sheep and ruled with an iron hand, much as his forbears had ruled in the valley. He also went into politics, learned to make a good stump speech and got himself elected to the highly congenial position of sheriff. In this place he made a great reputation for fearlessness and for the ruthless and skilful use of a gun. He once kicked down the locked door of a saloon and arrested ten armed gamblers, who had threatened to kill him. He was known and feared all over the territory and was a tyrant in his own section of it. When a gringo prospector ventured to dispute with him the ownership of a certain mine, the gringo was found dead in the bottom of the shaft. It was reported that he had fallen in and broken his neck and no one dared to look at the bullet hole in his back.

Don Diego's wife died without leaving him any children, but he had numerous children none-theless. It was said that one could follow his wanderings about the territory by the sporadic occurrence of the unmistakable Delcasar nose among the younger inhabitants. All of his sons and daughters by the left hand he treated with notable generosity. He was a sort of hero to the native people — a great fighter, a great lover — and songs about his adventures were composed and sung around the fires in sheep camps and by gangs of trackworkers.

Don Diego, in a word, was a true Delcasar and a great man. Had he used his opportunities wisely he might have been a millionaire. But at the age of sixty he owned little besides his house and his wild mountain lands. He drank a good deal and played poker almost every night. Once he had been a famous winner, but in these later years he generally lost. He also formed a partnership with a real estate broker named Mac-Dougall, for the development of his wild lands, and it was predicted by some that the leading development would be an ultimate transfer of title to Mr. MacDougall, who was known to be lending the Don money and taking land as security.

Don Felipe's career was far less spectacular than that of his brother. He owned more than Don Diego to start with, and he spent his life slowly losing it, so that when he died he left nothing but a house in Old Town and a single small sheep ranch, which afforded his widow, two daughters and one son a scant living.

This son, Ramon Delcasar, was the hope of

the family. He would inherit the estate of Don Diego, if the old Don died before spending it all, which it did not seem likely that he would do. But Ramon early demonstrated that he had a more important heritage in the sharp intelligence, and the proud, plucky and truculent spirit which had characterized the best of the Delcasars throughout the family history.

As there was no considerable family estate for him to settle upon, he was sent to law school at the age of twenty, and returned three years later to take up the practice of his profession in his native town. Thus he was the first of the Delcasars to face life with his bare hands. And he was also the last of them in a sense, to face the gringos. All the others of his name, save the senile Don, had either died, departed or sunk from sight into the mass of the peasantry.

CHAPTER III

The year that Ramon returned to his native town the annual fair, which took place at the fair-grounds in Old Town, was an especially gorgeous and throngful event, rich in spectacle and incident. A steer was roped and hog-tied in record time by Clay MacGarnigal of Lincoln County. A seven-mile relay race was won by a buck named Slonny Begay. In the bronco busting contest two men were injured to the huge enjoyment of the crowd. The twenty-seventh cavalry from Fort Bliss performed a sham battle. The home team beat several other teams. Enormous apples raised by irrigation in the Pecos Valley attracted much attention, and a hungry Mexican absconded with a prize Buff Orpington rooster.

Twice a day the single narrow street which connected the neat brick and frame respectability of New Town with the picturesque *adobe* squalor of Old Town was filled by a curiously varied crowd. The tourist from the East, distinguished by his camera and his unnecessary umbrella, jostled the Pueblo squaw from Isleta, with her latest-born slung over her shoulder in a fold of red blanket. Mexican families from the country marched in single file, the men first, then the women enveloped in huge black shawls, carrying babies and leading older children by the hand. Cowboys, Indians and soldiers raced their horses through the swarming street with reckless skill. Automobiles honked and fretted. The street cars, bulging humanity at every door and window, strove in vain to relieve the situation. Several children and numerous pigs and chickens were run over. From the unpaved street to the cloudless sky rose a vast cloud of dust, such as only a rainless country made of sand can produce. Dust was in every one's eyes and mouth and upon every one's clothing. It was the unofficial badge of the gathering. It turned the green of the cottonwood trees to grey, and lay in wait for unsuspecting teeth between the halves of hamburger sandwiches sold at corner booths.

Ramon, who had obtained a pass to the grounds through the influence of his uncle, went to the fair every day, although he was not really pleased with it. He was assured by every one that it was the greatest fair ever held in the southwest, but to him it seemed smaller, dustier and less exciting than the fairs he had attended in his boyhood.

This impression harmonized with a general feeling of discontent which had possessed him since his return. He had obtained a position in the office of a lawyer at fifty dollars a month, and spent the greater part of each day making out briefs and borrowing books for his employer from other lawyers. It seemed to him a petty and futile occupation, and the way to anything better was long and obscure. The town was full of other young lawyers who were doing the same things and doing them with a better grace than he. They were impelled by a great desire to make money. He, too, would have liked a great deal of money, but he had no taste for piling it up dollar by dollar. The only thing that cheered him was the prospect of inheriting his uncle's wealth, and that was an uncertain prospect. Don Diego seemed to be doing what he could to get rid of his property before he died.

Local society did not please Ramon either. The girls of the gringo families were not nearly as pretty, for the most part, as the ones he had seen in the East. The dryness and the scorching sun had a bad effect on their complexions. The girls of his own race did not much interest him; his liking was for blondes. And besides, girls were relatively scarce in the West because of the great number of men who came from the East. Competition for their favours was keen, and he could not compete successfully because he had so little money.

The fair held but one new experience for him,

and that was the Montezuma ball. This took place on the evening of the last day, and was an exclusive invitation event, designed to give elegance to the fair by bringing together prominent persons from all parts of the state. Ramon had never attended a Montezuma ball, as he had been considered a mere boy before his departure for college and had not owned a dress suit. But this lack had now been supplied, and he had obtained an invitation through the Governor of the State, who happened to be a Mexican.

He went to the ball with his mother and his eldest sister in a carriage which had been among the family possessions for about a quarter of a century. It had once been a fine equipage, and had been drawn by a spirited team in the days before Felipe Delcasar lost all his money, but now it had a look of decay, and the team consisted of a couple of rough coated, low-headed brutes, one of which was noticeably smaller than the other. The coachman was a ragged native who did odd jobs about the Delcasar house.

The Montezuma ball took place in the new Eldorado Hotel which had recently been built by the railroad company for the entertainment of its transcontinental passengers. It was not a beautiful building, but it was an apt expression of the town's personality. Designed in the ancient style of the early Spanish missions, long, low and sprawling, with deep verandahs, odd little towers and arched gateways it was made of cement and its service and prices were of the Manhattan school. A little group of Pueblo Indians, lonesomely picturesque in buck-skin and red blankets, with silver and turquoise rings and bracelets, were always seated before its doors, trying to sell fruit and pottery to well-tailored tourists. It had a museum of Southwestern antiquities and curios, where a Navajo squaw sulkily wove blankets on a handloom for the edification of the guilded stranger from the East. On the platform in front of it, perspiring Mexicans smashed baggage and performed the other hard labour of a modern terminal.

Thus the Eldorado Hotel was rich in that contrast between the old and the new which everywhere characterized the town. Generally speaking, the old was on exhibition or at work, while the new was at leisure or in charge.

When the Delcasar carriage reached the hotel, it had to take its place in a long line of crawling vehicles, most of which were motor cars. Ramon felt acutely humiliated to arrive at the ball in a decrepit-looking rig when nearly every one else came in an automobile. He hoped that no one would notice them. But the smaller of the two horses, which had spent most of his life in the

[29]

country, became frightened, reared, plunged, and finally backed the rig into one of the cars, smashing a headlight, blocking traffic, and making the Delcasars a target for searchlights and oaths. The Dona Delcasar, a ponderous and swarthy woman in voluminous black silk, became excited and stood up in the carriage, shouting shrill and useless directions to the coachman in Spanish. People began to laugh. Ramon roughly seized his mother by the arm and dragged her down. He was trembling with rage and embarassment.

It was an immense relief to him when he had deposited the two women on chairs and was able to wander away by himself. He took up his position in a doorway and watched the opening of the ball with a cold and disapproving eye. The beginning was stiff, for many of those present were unknown to each other and had little in common. Most of them were "Americans," Jews and Mexicans. The men were all a good deal alike in their dress suits, but the women displayed an astonishing variety. There were tall gawky blonde wives of prominent cattlemen; little natty black-eyed Jewesses, best dressed of all; swarthy Mexican mothers of politically important families, resplendent in black silk and diamonds; and pretty dark Mexican girls of the younger generation, who did not look at all like the señoritas of romance, but talked, dressed and flirted in a thoroughly American manner.

The affair finally got under way in the form of a grand march, which toured the hall a couple of times and disintegrated into waltzing couples. Ramon watched this proceeding and several other dances without feeling any desire to take part. He was in a state of grand and gloomy discontent, which was not wholly unpleasant, as is often the case with youthful glooms. He even permitted himself to smile at some of the capers cut by prominent citizens. But presently his gaze settled upon one couple with a real sense of resentment and uneasiness. The couple consisted of his uncle, Diego Delcasar, and the wife of James MacDougall, the lawyer and real estate operator with whom the Don had formed a partnership, and whom Ramon believed to be systematically fleecing the old man.

Don Diego was a big, paunchy Mexican with a smooth brown face, strikingly set off by fierce white whiskers. His partner was a tall, tight-lipped, angular woman, who danced painfully, but with determination. The two had nothing to say to each other, but both of them smiled resolutely, and the Don visibly perspired under the effort of steering his inflexible friend.

Although he did not formulate the idea, this

couple was to Ramon a symbol of the disgust with which the life of his native town inspired him. Here was the Mexican sedulously currying favour with the gringo, who robbed him for his pains. And here was the specific example of that relation which promised to rob Ramon of his heritage.

For the gringos he felt a cold hostility—a sense of antagonism and difference—but it was his senile and fatuous uncle, the type of his own defeated race, whom he despised.

CHAPTER IV

When the music stopped Ramon left the hall for the hotel lobby, where he soothed his sensibilities with a small brown cigarette of his own making. In one of the swinging benches covered with Navajo blankets two other dress-suited youths were seated, smoking and talking. One of them was a short, plump Jew with a round and gravely good-natured face; the other a tall, slender young fellow with a great mop of curly brown hair, large soft eyes and a sensitive mouth.

"She's good looking, all right," the little fellow assented, as Ramon came up.

"Good looking!" exclaimed the other with enthusiasm. "She's a little queen! Nothing like her ever hit this town before."

"Who's all the excitement about?" Ramon demanded, thrusting himself into the conversation with the easy familiarity which was his right as one of "the bunch."

Sidney Felberg turned to him in mock amazement.

"Good night, Ramon! Where have you been? Asleep? We're talking about Julia Roth, same as everybody else . . ."

"Who's she?" Ramon queried coolly, discharging a cloud of smoke from the depths of his lungs. "Never heard of her."

"Well, she's our latest social sensation . . . sister of some rich lunger that recently hit town; therefore very important. But that's not the only reason. Wait till you see her."

"All right; introduce me to her," Ramon suggested.

"Go on; knock him down to the lady," Sidney proposed to his companion.

"No, you," Conny demurred. "I refuse to take the responsibility. He's too good looking."

"All right," Sidney assented. "Come on. It's the only way I can get a look at her anyway—introducing somebody else. A good-looking girl in this town can start a regular stampede. We ought to import a few hundred. . . . ."

It was during an intermission. They forced their way through a phalanx of men brandishing programs and pencils, each trying to bring himself exclusively to the attention of a small blonde person who seemed to have some such quality of attractiveness for men as spilled honey has for insects.

When Ramon saw her he felt as though something inside of him had bumped up against his diaphragm, taking away his breath for a moment, agitating him strangely. And he saw an answering surprised recognition in her wide grey eyes.

"You ...you're the girl on the train," he remarked idiotically, as he took her hand.

She turned pink and laughed.

"You're the man that wouldn't look up," she mocked.

"What's all this about?" demanded Sidney. "You two met before?"

"May I have a dance?" Ramon inquired, suddenly recovering his presence of mind.

"Let me see . . . you're awfully late." They put their heads close together over her program. He saw her cut out the name of another man who had two dances, and then she held her pencil poised.

"Of course I didn't get your name," she admitted,

"No; I'll write it...Was it Carter? Delcasar? Ramon Delcasar. You must be Spanish. I was wondering . . . you're so dark. I'm awfully interested in Spanish people. . ." She wrote the name in a bold, upright, childish hand.

Ramon found that he had lost his mood of discontent after this, and he entered with zest into the spirit of the dance which was fast losing its stiff and formal character. Punch and music had broken down barriers. The hall was noisy with the ringing, high pitched laughter of excitement. It was warm and filled with an exotic, stimulating

[35]

odour, compounded of many perfumes and of perspiration. Every one danced. Young folk danced as though inspired, swaying their bodies in time to the tune. The old and the fat danced with pathetic joyful earnestness, going round and round the hall with red and perspiring faces, as though in this measure they might recapture youth and slimness if only they worked hard enough. Now and then a girl sang a snatch of the tune in a clear young voice, full of abandon, and sometimes others took up the song and it rose triumphant above the music of the orchestra for a moment, only to be lost again as the singers danced apart.

Ramon had been looking forward so long and with such intense anticipation to his dance with Julia Roth that he was a little self-conscious at its beginning, but this feeling was abolished by the discovery that they could dance together perfectly. He danced in silence, looking down upon her yellow head and white shoulders, the odour of her hair filling his nostrils, forgetful of everything but the sensuous delight of the moment.

This mood of solemn rapture was evidently not shared by her, for presently the yellow head was thrown back, and she smiled up at him a bit mockingly.

"Just like on the train," she remarked. "Not a thing to say for yourself. Are you always thus silent?"

[36]

Ramon grinned.

"No," he countered, "I was just trying to get up the nerve to ask if you'll let me come to see you."

"That doesn't take much nerve," she assured him. "Practically every man I've danced with tonight has asked me that. I never had so many dates before in my life."

"Well; may I follow the crowd, then?"

"You may," she laughed. "Or call me up first, and maybe there won't be any crowd."

CHAPTER V

His mother and sister had left early, for which fact he was thankful. He walked home alone with his hat in his hand, letting the cold wind of early morning blow on his hot brow. Punch and music and dancing had filled him with a delightful excitement. He felt glad of life and full of power. He could have gone on walking for hours, enjoying the rhythm of his stride and the gorgeous confusion of his thoughts, but in a remarkably short time he had covered the mile to his house in Old Town.

It was a long, low *adobe* with a paintless and rickety wooden verandah along its front, and with deep-set, iron-barred windows looking upon the square about which Old Town was built. Delcasars had lived in this house for over a century. Once it had been the best in town. Now it was an antiquity pointed out to tourists. Most of the Mexicans who had money had moved away from Old Town and built modern brick houses in New Town. But this was an expensive proceeding. The old *adobe* houses which they left brought them little. The Delcasars had never been able to afford this removal. They were deeply at-

[38]

tached to the old house and also deeply ashamed of it.

Ramon passed through a narrow hallway into a courtyard and across it to his room. The light of the oil lamp which he lit showed a large oblong chamber with a low ceiling supported by heavy timbers, whitewashed walls and heavy old-fashioned walnut furniture. A large coloured print of Mary and the Babe in a gilt frame hung over the wash-stand, and next to it a college pennant was tacked over a photograph of his graduating class. Several Navajo blankets covered most of the floor and a couple of guns stood in a corner.

When he was in bed his overstimulated state of mind became a torment. He rolled and tossed, beset by exciting images and ideas. Every time that a growing confusion of these indicated the approach of sleep, he was brought sharply back to full consciousness by the crowing of a rooster in the backyard. Finally he threw off the covers and sat up, cursing the rooster in two languages and resolving to eat him.

Sleep was out of the question now. Suddenly he remembered that this was Sunday morning, and that he had intended going to the mountains. To start at once would enable him to avoid an argument with his mother concerning the inevitability of damnation for those who miss early

Mass. He rose and dressed himself, putting on a cotton shirt, a faded and dirty pair of overalls and coarse leather riding boots; tied a red and white bandana about his neck and stuck on his head an old felt hat minus a band and with a drooping brim. So attired he looked exactly like a Mexican countryman—a poor *ranchero* or a woodcutter. This masquerade was not intentional nor was he conscious of it. He simply wore for his holiday the kind of clothes he had always worn about the sheep ranches.

Nevertheless he felt almost as different from his usual self as he looked. A good part of his identity as a poor, discontented and somewhat lazy young lawyer was hanging in the closet with his ready-made business suit. He took a long and noisy drink from the pitcher on the washstand, picked up his shot-gun and slipped cautiously out of the house, feeling care-free and happy.

Behind the house was a corral with an *adobe* wall that was ten feet high except where it had fallen down and been patched with boards. A scrub cow and three native horses were kept there. Two of the horses made the ill-matched team that hauled his mother and sister to church and town. The other was a fiery ragged little roan mare which he kept for his own use. None of these horses was worth more than thirty dollars, and they were easily kept on a few tons of alfalfa a year.

The little mare laid back her ears and turned as though to annihilate him with a kick. He quickly stepped right up against the threatening hind legs, after the fashion of experienced horsemen who know that a kick is harmless at short range, and laid his hand on her side. She trembled but dared not move. He walked to her head, sliding his hand along the rough, uncurried belly and talking to her in Spanish. In a moment he had the bridle on her.

The town was impressively empty and still as he galloped through it. Hoof beats rang out like shots, scaring a late-roaming cat, which darted across the street like a runaway shadow.

Near the railroad station he came to a large white van, with a beam of light emerging from its door. This was a local institution of long-standing, known as the chile-wagon, and was the town's only all-night resturant. Here he aroused a fat, sleepy old Mexican.

"*Un tamale y cafe*," he ordered, and then had the proprietor make him a couple of sandwiches to put in his pocket. He consumed his breakfast hurriedly, rolled and lit a little brown cigarette, and was off again.

His way led up a long steep street lined with new houses and vacant lots; then out upon the high empty level of the *mesa*. It was daylight now, of a clear, brilliant morning. He was riding across a level prairie, which was a grey desert most of the year, but which the rainy season of late summer had now touched with rich colours. The grass in many of the hollows was almost high enough to cut with a scythe, and its green expanse was patched with purple-flowered weeds. Meadow larks bugled from the grass; flocks of wild doves rose on whistling wings from the weed patches; a great grey jack-rabbit with jet-tipped ears sprang from his form beside the road and went sailing away in long effortless bounds, like a wind-blown thing. Miles ahead were the mountains—an angular mass of blue distance and purple shadow, rising steep five thousand feet above the *mesa,* with little round foothills clustering at their feet. A brisk cool wind fanned his face and fluttered the brim of his hat.

But with the rising of the sun the wind dropped, it became warm and he felt dull and sleepy. When he came to a little juniper bush which spread its bit of shadow beside the road, he dismounted, pulled the saddle off his sweating mare, and sat down in the shade to eat his lunch. When he had finished he wished for a drink of water and philosophically took a smoke instead. Then he lay down, using his saddle for a pillow, puffing luxuriously at his cigarette. It was cool in his bit of shadow, though all the world about him swam in waves of heat. . . . Cool and very quiet. He felt drowsily content. This sunny desolation was to him neither lonely nor beautiful; it was just his own country, the soil from which he had sprung. . . . Colours and outlines blurred as his eyelids grew heavy. Sleep conquered him in a sudden black rush.

It was late afternoon when he awakened. He had meant to shoot doves, but it was too late now to do any hunting if he was to reach Archulera's place before dark. He saddled his mare hurriedly and went forward at a hard gallop.

Archulera's place was typical of the little Mexican ranches that dot the Southwest wherever there is water enough to irrigate a few acres. The brown block of *adobe* house stood on an arid, rocky hillside, and looked like a part of it, save for the white door, and a few bright scarlet strings of *chile* hung over the rafter ends to dry. Down in the *arroyo* was the little fenced patch where corn and *chile* and beans were raised, and behind the house was a round goat corral of wattled brush. The skyward rocky waste of the mountain lifted behind the house, and the empty reach of the *mesa* lay before—an immense and arid loneliness, now softened and beautified by many shadows.

Ramon could see old man Archulera far up the

mountainside, rounding up his goats for evening milking, and he could faintly hear the bleating of the animals and the old man's shouts and imprecations. He whistled loudly through his fingers and waved his hat.

"Como lo va primo!" he shouted, and he saw Archulera stop and look, and heard faintly his answering, *"Como la va!"*

Soon Archulera had his goats penned, and Ramon joined him while he milked half a dozen ewes.

"I'm glad you came," Archulera told him, "I haven't seen a man in a month except one gringo that said he was a prospector and stole a kid from me.... How was the fair?"

When the milking was over, the old man selected a fat kid, caught it by the hind leg and dragged it, bleating in wild terror, to a gallows behind the house, where he hung it up and skilfully cut its throat, leaving it to bleat and bleed to death while he wiped his knife and went on talking volubly with his guest. The occasional visits of Ramon were the most interesting events in his life, and he always killed a kid to express his appreciation. Ramon reciprocated with gifts of tobacco and whisky. They were great friends.

Archulera was a short, muscular Mexican with a swarthy, wrinkled face, broad but well-cut. His big, thin-lipped mouth showed an amazing disarray of strong yellow teeth when he smiled. His little black eyes were shrewd and full of fire. Although he was sixty years old, there was little grey in the thick black hair that hung almost to his shoulders. He wore a cheap print shirt and a faded pair of overalls, belted at the waist with a strip of red wool. His foot-gear consisted of the uppers of a pair of old shoes with soles of rawhide sewed on moccasin-fashion.

With no more disguise than a red blanket and a grunt Archulera could have passed for an Indian anywhere, but he made it clear to all that he regarded himself as a Spanish gentleman. He was descended, like Ramon, from one of the old families, which had received occasional infusions of native blood. There was probably more Indian in him than in the young man, but the chief difference between the two was due to the fact that the Archuleras had lost most of their wealth a couple of generations before, so that the old man had come down in the social scale to the condition of an ordinary goat-herding *pelado*. There are many such fallen aristocrats among the New Mexican peasantry. Most of them, like Archulera, are distinguished by their remarkably choice and fluent use of the Spanish language, and by the formal, eighteenth-century perfection of their manners, which contrast strangely with the barbaric way of their lives.

The old man was now skinning and butchering the goat with speed and skill. Nothing was wasted. The hide was flung over a rafter end to dry. The head was washed and put in a pan, as were the smaller entrails with bits of fat clinging to them, and the liver and heart. The meat was too fresh to be eaten tonight, but these things would serve well enough for supper, and he called to his daughter, Catalina, to come and get them.

The two men soon joined her in the low, white-washed room, which had hard mud for a floor, and was furnished with a bare table and a few chairs. It was clean, but having only one window and that always closed, it had a pronounced and individual odour. In one corner was a little fire-place, which had long served both for cooking and to furnish heat, but as a concession to modern ideas Archulera had lately supplemented it with a cheap range in the opposite corner. There Catalina was noisily distilling an aroma from goat liver and onions. The entrails she threaded on little sticks and broiled them to a delicate brown over the coals, while the head she placed whole in the oven. Later this was cracked open and the brains taken out with a spoon, piping hot and very savoury. These viands were supplemented by a pan of large pale biscuits, and a big tin pot of coffee. Catalina served the two men, saying nothing, not even raising her eyes, while they talked and paid no attention to her. After eating her own supper and washing the dishes she disappeared into the next room.

This self-effacing behaviour on the part of the girl accorded with the highest standards of Mexican etiquette, and showed her good breeding. The fact that old Archulera paid no more attention to her than to a chair did not indicate that he was indifferent to her. On the contrary, as Ramon had long ago discovered, she was one of the chief concerns of his life. He could not forget that in her veins flowed some of the very best of Spanish blood, and he considered her altogether too good for the common sheep-herders and wood-cutters who aspired to woo her. These he summarily warned away, and brought his big Winchester rifle into the argument whenever it became warm. When he left the girl alone, in order to guard her from temptation he locked her into the house together with his dog. Catalina had led a starved and isolated existence.

After the meal, Archulera became reminiscent of his youth. Some thirty-five years before he had been one of the young bloods of the country, having fought against the Navajos and Apaches. He had made a reputation, long since forgotten by every one but himself, for ruthless courage and straight shooting, and many a man had he killed. In his early life, as he had often told

Ramon, he had been a boon companion of old
Diego Delcasar. The two had been associated
in some mining venture, and Archulera claimed
that Delcasar had cheated him out of his share of
the proceeds, and so doomed him to his present
life of poverty. When properly stimulated by
food and drink Archulera never failed to tell this
story, and to express his hatred for the man who
had deprived him of wealth and social position.
He had at first approached the subject diffidently,
not knowing how Ramon would regard an attack
on the good name of his uncle, and being anxious
not to offend the young man. But finding that
Ramon listened tolerantly, if not sympathetically,
he had told the story over and over, each time
with more detail and more abundant and picturesque denunciation of Diego Delcasar, but with
substantial uniformity as to the facts. As he
spoke he watched the face of Ramon narrowly.
Always the recital ended about the same way.

"You are not like your uncle," he assured the
young man earnestly, in his formal Spanish.
"You are generous, honourable. When your
uncle is dead, you will repay me for the wrongs
that I have suffered—no?"

Ramon would always laugh at this. This night,
in order to humour the old man, he asked him how
much he thought the Delcasar estate owed him
for his ancient wrong.

[48]

"Five thousand dollars!" Archulera replied with slow emphasis. He probably had no idea how much he had lost, but five thousand dollars was his conception of a great deal of money.

Ramon again laughed and refused to commit himself. He certainly had no idea of giving Archulera five thousand dollars, but he thought that if he ever did come into his own he would certainly take care of the old man—and of Catalina.

Soon after this Archulera went off to sleep in the other end of the house, after trying in vain to persuade Ramon to occupy his bed. Ramon, as always, refused. He would sleep on a pile of sheep skins in the corner. He really preferred this, because the sheep skins were both cleaner and softer than Archulera's bed, and also for another reason.

After the old man had gone, he stretched out on his pallet, and lit another cigarette. He could hear his host thumping around for a few minutes; then it was very still, save for a faint moan of wind and the ticking of a cheap clock. This late still hour had always been to him one of the most delightful parts of his visits to Archulera's house. For some reason he got a sense of peace and freedom out of this far-away quiet place. And he knew that in the next room Catalina was waiting for him—Catalina with the strong, shapely brown body which her formless calico smock concealed by day, with the eager, blind desire bred of her long loneliness.

During his first few visits to Archulera, he had scarcely noticed the girl. That was doubtless one reason why the old man had welcomed him. He had come here simply to go deer-hunting with Archulera, to eat his goat meat and chile, to get away from the annoyance and boredom of his life in town, and into the crude, primitive atmosphere which he had loved as a boy. Catalina had been to him just the usual slovenly figure of a Mexican woman, a self-effacing drudge.

He had felt her eyes upon him several times, had not looked up quickly enough to meet them, but had noticed the pretty soft curve of her cheek. Then one night when he was stretched out on his sheep skins after Archulera had gone to bed, the girl came into the room and began pottering about the stove. He had watched her, wondering what she was doing. As she knelt on the floor he noticed the curve of her hip, the droop of her breast against her frock, the surprising round perfection of her outstretched arm. It struck him suddenly that she was a woman to be desired, and one who might be taken with ease. At the same time, with a quickening of the blood, he realized that she was doing nothing, and had merely come into the room to attract his attention. Then she glanced at him, daring but shy, with great brown eyes, like the eyes of a gentle animal. When she went back to her own room a moment later, he confidently followed.

Ever since then Catalina had been the chief object of his week-end journeys, and his hunting largely an excuse. She had completed this life which he led in the mountains, and which was so pleasantly different from his life in town. For a part of the week he was a poor, young lawyer, watchful, worried, careful; then for a couple of days he was a ragged young Mexican and the lover of Catalina—a different man. He was the product of a transition, and two beings warred in him. In town he was dominated by the desire to be like the Americans, and to gain a foothold in their life of law, greed and respectability; in the mountains he relapsed unconsciously into the easy barbarous ways of his fathers. Incidentally, this periodical change of personality was refreshing and a source of strength. Catalina had been an important part of it. . . . As he lay now sleepily puffing a last cigarette, he wondered why it was that he had suddenly lost interest in the girl.

CHAPTER VI

At ten o'clock in the morning Ramon was hard at work in the office of James B. Green. He worked efficiently and with zest as he always did after one of his trips to the mountains. He got out of these ventures into another environment about what some men get out of sprees—a complete change of the state of mind. Archulera and his daughter were now completely forgotten, and all of his usual worries and plans were creeping back into his consciousness.

But this day he had a feeling of pleasant anticipation. At first he could not account for it. And then he remembered the girl—the one he had seen on the train and had met again at the Montezuma ball. It seemed as though the thought of her had been in the back of his mind all the time, and now suddenly came forward, claiming all his attention, stirring him to a quick, unwonted excitement. She had said he might come to see her. He was to 'phone first. Maybe she would be alone. . . .

In this latter hope he was disappointed. She gave him the appointment, and she herself admitted him. He thought he had never seen such a dainty bit of fragrant perfection, all in pink that matched the pink of her strange little crinkled mouth.

"I'm awfully glad you came," she told him. (Her gladness was always awful.) She led him into the sitting room and presented him to the tall emaciated sick man and the large placid woman who had watched over her so carefully on the train.

Gordon Roth greeted him with a cool and formal manner into which he evidently tried to infuse something of cordiality, as though a desire to be just and broad-minded struggled with prejudice. Mrs. Roth looked at him with curiosity, and gave him a still more restrained greeting. The conversation was a weak and painful affair, kept barely alive, now by one and now by another. The atmosphere was heavy with disapproval. If their greetings had left Ramon in any doubt as to the attitude of the girl's family toward him, that doubt was removed by the fact that neither Mrs. Roth nor her son showed any intention of leaving the room. This would have been not unusual if he had called on a Mexican girl, especially if she belonged to one of the more old-fashioned families; but he knew that American girls are left alone with their suitors if the suitor is at all welcome.

He knew a little about this family from hearsay. They came from one of the larger factory towns in northern New York, and were supposed to be moderately wealthy. They used a very broad "a" and served tea at four o'clock in the afternoon. Gordon Roth was a Harvard graduate and did not conceal the fact. Neither did he conceal his hatred for this sandy little western town, where ill-health had doomed him to spend many of his days and perhaps to end them.

The girl was strangely different from her mother and brother. Whereas their expressions were stiff and solemn, her eyes showed an irrepressible gleam of humour, and her fascinating little mouth was mobile with mirth. She fidgeted around in her chair a good deal, as a child does when bored.

Mrs. Roth decorously turned the conversation toward the safe and reliable subjects of literature and art.

"What do you think of Maeterlinck, Mr. Delcasar?" she enquired in an innocent manner that must have concealed malice.

"I don't know him," Ramon admitted, "Who is he?"

Mrs. Roth permitted herself to smile. Gordon Roth came graciously to the rescue.

"Maeterlinck is a great Belgian writer," he explained. "We are all very much interested in him...."

Julia gave a little flounce in her chair, and crossed her legs with a defiant look at her mother.

"I'm not interested in him," she announced with decision. "I think he's a bore. Listen, Mr. Delcasar. You know Conny Masters? Well, he was telling me the most thrilling tale the other day. He said that the country Mexicans have a sort of secret religious fraternity that most of the men belong to, and that they meet every Good Friday and beat themselves with whips and sit down on cactus and crucify a man on a cross and all sorts of horrible things . . . for penance you know, just like the monks and things in the Middle Ages. . . . He claims he saw them once and that they had blood running down to their heels. Is that all true? I've forgotten what he called them. . . ."

Ramon nodded.

"Sure. The *penitentes*. I've seen them lots of times."

"O, do tell us about them. I love to hear about horrible things."

"Well, I've seen lots of *penitente* processions, but the best one I ever saw was a long time ago, when I was a little kid. There are not so many of them now, and they don't do as much as they used to. The church is down on them, you know, and they're afraid. Ten years ago if you tried

[55]

to look at them, they would shoot at you, but now tourists take pictures of them."

Gordon Roth's curiosity had been aroused.

"Tell me," he broke in. "What is the meaning of this thing? How did it get started?"

"I don't know exactly," Ramon admitted. "My grandfather told me that they brought it over from Spain centuries ago, and the Indians here had a sort of whipping fraternity, and the two got mixed up, I guess. The church used to tolerate it; it was a regular religious festival. But now it's outlawed. They still have a lot of political power. They all vote the same way. One man that was elected to Congress—they say that the *penitente* stripes on his back carried him there. And he was a gringo too. But I don't know. It may be a lie. . . ."

"But tell us about that procession you saw when you were a little boy," Julia broke in. She was leaning forward with her chin in her hand, and her big grey eyes, wide with interest, fixed upon his face.

"Well, I was only about ten years old, and I was riding home from one of our ranches with my father. We were coming through *Tijeras* canyon. It was March, and there was snow on the ground in patches, and the mountains were cold and bare, and I remember I thought I was going to freeze. Every little while we would get off and set fire to

a tumble-weed by the road, and warm our hands
and then go on again. . . .

"Anyway, pretty soon I heard a lot of men singing, all together, in deep voices, and the noise
echoed around the canyon and sounded awful solemn. And I could hear, too, the slap of the big
wide whips coming down on the bare backs, wet
with blood, like slapping a man with a wet towel,
only louder. I didn't know what it was, but my
father did, and he called to me and we spurred
our horses right up the mountain, and hid in a
clump of cedar up there. Then they came around
a bend in the road, and I began to cry because
they were all covered with blood, and one of them
fell down. . . . My father slapped me and told
me to shut up, or they would come and shoot us."

"But what did they look like? What were
they doing?" Julia demanded frowning at him,
impatient with his rambling narrative.

"Well, in front there was *un carreta del muerto*.
That means a wagon of death. I don't think you
would ever see one any more. It was just an ordinary wagon drawn by six men, naked to the
waist and bleeding, with other men walking beside
them and beating them with blacksnake whips,
just like they were mules. In the wagon they had
a big bed of stones, covered with cactus, and a man
sitting in the cactus, who was supposed to rep-
resent death. And then they had a Virgin Mary,

[57]

too. Four *penitentes* just like the others, with nothing on but bloody pants and black bandages around their eyes, carried the image on a litter raised up over their heads, and they had swords fastened to their elbows and stuck between their ribs, so that if they let down, the swords would stick into their hearts and kill them. And behind that came the *Cristo*—the man that represented Jesus, you know, dragging a big cross. Behind him came twenty or thirty more *penitentes,* the most I ever saw at once, some of them whipping themselves with big broad whips made out of *amole*. One was too weak to whip himself, so two others walked behind him and whipped him. Pretty soon he fell down and they walked over him and stepped on his stomach. . . ."

"But did they crucify the man, the whatever-you-call-him?" Gordon demanded.

"The *Cristo*. Sure. They crucify one every year. They used to nail him. Now they generally do it with ropes, but that's bad enough, because it makes him swell up and turn blue. . . . Sometimes he dies."

Julia was listening with lips parted and eyes wide, horrified and yet fascinated, as are so many women by what is cruel and bloody. But Gordon, who had become equally interested, was cool and inquisitive.

"And you mean to tell me that at one time

[58]

nearly all the—er—native people belonged to this barbaric organization, and that many of them do yet?"

"Nearly all the common *pelados*," Ramon hastened to explain. "They are nearly all Indian or part Indian, you know. Not the educated people." Here a note of pride came into his voice. "We are descended from officers of the Spanish army—the men who conquered this country. In the old days, before the Americans came, all these common people were our slaves."

"I see," said Gordon Roth in a dry and judicial tone.

The *penitentes*, as a subject of conversation, seemed exhausted for the time being and Ramon had given up all hope of being alone with Julia. He rose and took his leave. To his delight Julia followed him to the door. In the hall she gave him her hand and looked up at him, and neither of them found anything to say. For some reason the pressure of her hand and the look of her eyes flustered and confused him more than had all the coldness and disapproval of her family. At last he said good-bye and got away, with his hat on wrong side before and the blood pounding in his temples.

CHAPTER VII

During the following weeks Ramon worked even less than was his custom. He also neglected his trips to the mountains and most of his other amusements. They seemed to have lost their interest for him. But he was a regular attendant upon the weekly dances which were held at the country club, and to which he had never gone before.

The country club was a recent acquisition of the town, backed by a number of local business men. It consisted of a picturesque little frame lodge far out upon the *mesa,* and a nine-hole golf course, made of sand and haunted by lizzards and rattlesnakes. It had become a centre of local society, although there was a more exclusive organization known as the Forty Club, which gave a formal ball once a month. Ramon had never been invited to join the Forty Club, but the political importance of his family had procured him a membership in the country club and it served his present purpose very well, for he found Julia Roth there every Saturday night. This fact was the sole reason for his going. His dances with her were now the one thing in life to which he looked forward with pleasure, and his highest hope was that he might be alone with her.

In this he was disappointed for a long time because Julia was the belle of the town. Her dainty, provocative presence seemed always to be the centre of the gathering. Women envied her and studied her frocks, which were easily the most stylish in town. Men flocked about her and guffawed at her elfin stabs of humour. Her program was always crowded with names, and when she went for a stroll between dances she was generally accompanied by at least three men of whom Ramon was often one. And while the others made her laugh at their jokes or thrilled her with accounts of their adventures, he was always silent and worried—an utter bore, he thought.

This girl was a new experience to him. With the egotism of twenty-four, he had regarded himself as a finished man of the world, especially with regard to women. They had always liked him. He was good to look at and his silent, self-possessed manner touched the feminine imagination. He had had his share of the amorous adventures that come to most men, and his attitude toward women had changed from the hesitancy of adolescence to the purposeful, confident and somewhat selfish attitude of the male accustomed to easy conquest.

[61]

This girl, by a smile and touch of her hand, seemed to have changed him. She filled him with a mighty yearning. He desired her, and yet there was a puzzling element in his feeling that seemed to transcend desire. And he was utterly without his usual confidence and purpose. He had reason enough to doubt his success, but aside from that she loomed in his imagination as something high and unattainable. He had no plan. His strength seemed to have oozed out of him. He pursued her persistently enough—in fact too persistently—but he did it because he could not help it.

The longer he followed in her wake, the more marked his weakness became. When he approached her to claim a dance he was often aware of a faint tremble in his knees, and was embarrassed by the fact that the palms of his hands were sweating. He felt that he was a fool and swore at himself. And he was wholly unable to believe that he was making any impression upon her. True, she was quite willing to flirt with him. She looked up at him with an arch, almost enquiring glance when he came to claim her for a dance, but he seldom found much to say at such times, being too wholly absorbed in the sacred occupation of dancing with her. And it seemed to him that she flirted with every one else, too. This did not in the least mitigate his devotion, but it made him acutely uncomfortable to watch her dance with other men, and especially with Conny Masters.

Masters was the son of a man who had made a moderate fortune in the tin-plate business. He had come West with his mother who had a weak throat, had fallen in love with the country, and scandalized his family by resolutely refusing to go back to Indiana and tin cans. He spent most of his time riding about the country, equipped with a note book and a camera, studying the Mexicans and Indians, and taking pictures of the scenery. He said that he was going to make a literary career, but the net product of his effort for two years had been a few sonnets of lofty tone but vague meaning, and a great many photographs, mostly of sunsets.

Conny was not a definite success as a writer, but he was unquestionably a gifted talker, and he knew the country better than did most of the natives. He made real to Julia the romance which she craved to find in the West. And her watchful and suspicious family seemed to tolerate if not to welcome him. Ramon knew that he went to the Roth's regularly. He began to feel something like hatred for Conny whom he had formerly liked.

This feeling was deepened by the fact that Conny seemed to be specially bent on defeating

Ramon's ambition to be alone with the girl. If no one else joined them at the end of a dance, Conny was almost sure to do so, and to occupy the intermission with one of his ever-ready monologues, while Ramon sat silent and angry, wondering what Julia saw to admire in this windy fool, and occasionally daring to wonder whether she really saw anything in him after all.

But a sufficiently devoted lover is seldom wholly without a reward. There came an evening when Ramon found himself alone with her. And he was aware with a thrill that she had evaded not only Conny, but two other men. Her smile was friendly and encouraging, too, and yet he could not find anything to say which in the least expressed his feelings.

"Are you going to stay in this country long?" he began. The question sounded supremely casual, but it meant a great deal to him. He was haunted by a fear that she would depart suddenly, and he would never see her again. She smiled and looked away for a moment before replying, as though perhaps this was not exactly what she had expected him to say.

"I don't know. Gordon wants mother and me to go back East this fall, but I don't want to go and mother doesn't want to leave Gordon alone.... We haven't decided. Maybe I won't go till next year."

"I suppose you'll go to college won't you?"

"No; I wanted to go to Vassar and then study art, but mother says college spoils a girl for society. She thinks the way the Vassar girls walk is perfectly dreadful. I offered to go right on walking the same way, but she said anyway college makes girls so frightfully broad-minded. . . ."

Ramon laughed.

"What will you do then?"

"I'll come out."

"Out of what?"

"Make my début, don't you know?"

"O, yes."

"In New York. I have an aunt there. She knows all the best people, mother says."

"What happens after you come out?"

"You get married if anybody will have you. If not, you sort of fade away and finally go into uplift work about your fourth season."

"But of course, you'll get married. I bet you'll marry a millionaire."

"I don't know. Mother wants me to marry a broker. She says the big financial houses in New York are conducted by the very best people. But Gordon thinks I ought to marry a professional man—a doctor or something. He thinks brokers are vulgar. He says money isn't everything."

"What do you think?"

"I haven't a thought to my name. All my thinking has been done for me since infancy. I don't know what I want, but I'm pretty sure I wouldn't get it if I did. . . . Come on. They've been dancing for ten minutes. If we stay here any longer it'll be a scandal."

She rose and started for the hall. He suddenly realized that his long-sought opportunity was slipping away from him. He caught her by the hand.

"Don't go, please. I want to tell you something."

She met his hand with a fair grip, and pulled him after her with a laugh.

"Some other time," she promised.

CHAPTER VIII.

In most of their social diversions the town folk tended always more and more to ape the ways of the East. Local colour, they thought, was all right in its place, which was a curio store or a museum, but they desired their town to be modern and citified, so that the wealthy eastern health-seeker would find it a congenial home. The scenery and the historic past were recognized as assets, but they should be the background for a life of "culture, refinement and modern convenience" as the president of the Chamber of Commerce was fond of saying.

Hence the riding parties and picnics of a few years before had given way to aggressively formal balls and receptions; but one form of entertainment that was indigenous had survived. This was known as a *"mesa* supper." It might take place anywhere in the surrounding wilderness of mountain and desert. Several auto-loads of young folk would motor out, suitably chaperoned and laden with provisions. Beside some water hole or mountain stream fires would be built, steaks broiled and coffee brewed. Afterward there would be singing and story-telling about the fire, and romantic strolls by couples.

It was one of these expeditions that furnished Ramon with his second opportunity in three weeks to be alone with Julia Roth. The party had journeyed to Los Ojuellos, where a spring of clear water bubbled up in the centre of the *mesa*. A grove of cottonwood trees shadowed the place, and there was an ancient *adobe* ruin which looked especially effective by moonlight.

The persistent Conny Masters was a member of the party, but he was handicapped by the fact that he knew more about camp cookery than anyone else present. He had made a special study of Mexican dishes and had written an article about them which had been rejected by no less than twenty-seven magazines. He made a specialty of the *enchilada,* which is a delightful concoction of corn meal, eggs and chile, and he had perfected a recipe of his own for this dish which he had named the Conny Masters junior.

As soon as the baskets were unpacked and the chaperones were safely anchored on rugs and blankets with their backs against trees, there was a general demand, strongly backed by Ramon, that Conny should cook supper. He was soon absorbed in the process, volubly explaining every step, while the others gathered about him and offered encouragement and humorous suggestion. But there was soon a gradual dispersion of the group, some going for wood and some for water, and others on errands unstated.

Ramon found himself strolling under the cottonwoods with Julia. Neither of them had said anything. It was almost as though the tryst had been agreed upon before. She picked her way slowly among the tussocks of dried grass, her skirt daintily kilted. A faint but potent perfume from her hair and dress blew over him. He ventured to support her elbow with a reverent touch. Never had she seemed more desirable, nor yet, for some reason, more remote.

Suddenly she stopped and looked up at the great desert stars.

"Isn't it big and beautiful?" she demanded. "And doesn't it make you feel free? It's never like this at home, somehow."

"What is it like where you live?" he enquired. He had a persistent desire to see into her life and understand it, but everything she told him only made her more than ever to him a being of mysterious origin and destiny.

"It's a funny little New York factory city with very staid ways," she said. "You go to a dance at the country club every Saturday night and to tea parties and things in between. You fight, bleed and die for your social position and once in a while you stop and wonder why. . . . It's a bore. You can see yourself going on doing the same thing till the day of your death. . . ."

Her discontent with things as they are found ready sympathy.

"That's just the way it is here," he said with conviction. "You can't see anything ahead."

"Oh, I don't think its the same here at all," she protested. "This country's so big and interesting. It's different."

"Tell me how," he demanded. "I haven't seen anything interesting here since I got back,—except you."

She ignored the exception.

"I can't express it exactly. The people here are just like people everywhere else—most of them. But the country looks so big and unoccupied. And blue mountains are so alluring. There might be anything beyond them . . . adventures, opportunities. . . ."

This idea was a bit too rarefied for Ramon, but he could agree about the mountains.

"It's a fine country," he assented. "For those that own it."

"It's just a feeling I have about it," she went on, trying to express her own half-formulated idea. "But then I have that feeling about life in general, and there doesn't seem to be anything in it. I mean the feeling that it's full of thrilling things, but somehow you miss them all."

"I have felt something like that," he admitted. "But I never could say it."

This discovery of an idea in common seemed somehow to bring them closer together. His hand tightened gently about her arm; almost unconsciously he drew her toward him. But she seemed to be all absorbed in the discussion.

"You have no right to complain," she told him. "A man can do something about it."

"Yes," he agreed, speaking a reflection without stopping to put it in conventional language. "It must be hell to be a woman . . . excuse me . . . I mean. . . ."

"Don't apologize. It is—just that. A man at least has a fighting chance to escape boredom. But they won't even let a woman fight. I wish I were a man."

"Well; I don't," he asserted with warmth, unconsciously tightening his hold upon her arm. "I can't tell you how glad I am that you're a woman."

"Oh, are you?" She looked up at him with challenging, provocative eyes.

For an instant a kiss was imminent. It hovered between them like an invisible fairy presence

[71]

of which they both were sweetly aware, and no one else.

"Hey there! all you spooners!" came a jovial and irreverent voice from the vicinity of the camp fire. "Come and eat."

The moment was lost; the fairy presence gone. She turned with a little laugh, and they went in silence back to the fire. They were last to enter the circle of ruddy light, and all eyes were upon them. She was pink and self-conscious, looking at her feet and picking her way with exaggerated care. He was proud and elated. This, he knew, would couple their names in gossip, would make her partly his.

CHAPTER IX

He wanted to call on her again, but he felt that he had been insulted and rejected by the Roths, and his pride fought against it. Unable to think for long of anything but Julia he fell into the habit of walking by her house at night, looking at its lighted windows and wondering what she was doing. Often he could see the moving figures and hear the laughter of some gay group about her, but he could not bring himself to go in and face the chilly disapproval of her family. At such times he felt an utter outcast, and sounded depths of misery he had never known before. For this was his first real love, and he loved in the helpless, desperate way of the Latin, without calculation or humour.

One evening there was a gathering on the porch of the Roth house. She was there, sitting on the steps with three men about her. He could see the white blur of her frock and hear her funny little bubbling laugh above the deeper voices of the men. Having ascertained that neither Gordon Roth nor his mother was there, he summoned his courage and went in. She could not see who he was until he stood almost over her.

"O, it's you! I'm awfully glad. . . ." Their hands met and clung for a moment in the darkness. He sat down on the steps at her feet, and the conversation moved on without any assistance from him. He was now just as happy as he had been miserable a few minutes before.

Presently two of the other men went away, but the third, who was Conny Masters, stayed. He talked volubly as ever, telling wonderful and sometimes incredible stories of things he had seen and done in his wanderings. Ramon said nothing. Julia responded less and less. Once she moved to drop the wrap from about her shoulders, and the alert Conny hastened to assist her. Ramon watched and envied with a thumping heart as he saw the gleam of her bare white shoulders, and realized that his rival might have touched them.

Conny went on talking for half an hour with astonishing endurance and resourcefulness, but it became always more apparent that he was not captivating his audience. He had to laugh at his own humour and expatiate on his own thrills. Finally a silence fell upon the three, broken only by occasional commonplace remarks.

"Well, I guess it's time to drift," Conny observed at last, looking cautiously at his watch.

This suggestion was neither seconded by Ramon nor opposed by Julia. The silence literally pushed Conny to his feet.

"Going, Ramon? No? Well, Good night." And he retired whistling in a way which showed his irritation more plainly than if he had sworn.

The two impolite ones sat silent for a long moment. Ramon was trying to think of what he wanted to say and how he wanted to say it. Finally without looking at her he said in a low husky voice.

"You know . . . I love you."

There was more silence. At last he looked up and met her eyes. They were serious for the first time in his experience, and so was her usually mocking little mouth. Her face was transformed and dignified. More than ever she seemed a strange, high being. And yet he knew that now she was within his reach. . . . That he could kiss her lips . . . incredible. . . . And yet he did, and the kiss poured flame over them and welded them into each others' arms.

They heard Gordon Roth in the house coughing, the cough coming closer.

She pushed him gently away.

"Go now," she whispered. "I love you... Ramon."

CHAPTER X

His conquest was far from giving him peace.
Her kiss had transformed his high vague yearning into hot relentless desire. He wanted her.
That became the one clear thing in life to him.
Reflections and doubts were alien to his young
and primitive spirit. He did not try to look far
into the future. He only knew that to have her
would be delight almost unimaginable and to lose
her would be to lose everything.

His attitude toward her changed. He claimed
her more and more at dances. She did not
want to dance with him so much because "people
would talk," but his will was harder than hers
and to a great extent he had his way. He now
called on her regularly too. He knew that she
had fought hard for him against her family, and
had won the privilege for him of calling "not too
often."

"I 've lied for you frightfully," she confessed.
"I told them I didn't really care for you in the
least, but I want to see you because you can tell
such wonderful things about the country. So talk
about the country whenever they're listening.
And don 't look at me the way you do...."

Mother and brother were alert and suspicious despite her assurance, and manœuvred with cool skill to keep the pair from being alone. Only rarely did he get the chance to kiss her—once when her brother, who was standing guard over the family treasure, was seized with a fit of coughing and had to leave the room, and again when her mother was called to the telephone. At such times she shrank away from him at first as though frightened by the intensity of the emotion she had created, but she never resisted. To him these brief and stolen embraces were almost intolerably sweet, like insufficient sips of water to a man burned up with thirst.

She puzzled him as much as ever. When he was with her he felt as sure of her love as of his own existence. And yet she often sought to elude him. When he called up for engagements she objected and put him off. And she surrounded herself with other men as much as ever, and flirted gracefully with all of them, so that he was always feeling the sharp physical pangs of jealousy. Sometimes he felt egotistically sure that she was merely trying by these devices to provoke his desire the more, but at other times he thought her voice over the phone sounded doubtful and afraid, and he became wildly eager to get to her and make sure of her again.

Just as her kiss had crystallized his feeling for

her into driving desire, so it had focussed and intensified his discontent. Before he had been more or less resigned to wait for his fortune and the power he meant to make of it; now it seemed to him that unless he could achieve these things at once, they would never mean anything to him. For money was the one thing that would give him even a chance to win her. It was obviously useless to ask her to marry him poor. He would have nothing to bring against the certain opposition of her family. He could not run away with her. And indeed he was altogether too poor to support a wife if he had one, least of all a wife who had been carefully groomed and trained to capture a fortune.

There was only one way. If he could go to her strong and rich, he felt sure that he could persuade her to go away with him, for he knew that she belonged to him when he was with her. He pictured himself going to her in a great motor car. Such a car had always been in his imagination the symbol of material strength. He felt sure he could destroy her doubts and hesitations. He would carry her away and she would be all and irrevocably his before any one could interfere or object.

This dream filled and tortured his imagination. Its realization would mean not only fulfilment of his desire, but also revenge upon the Roths for the humiliations they had made him feel. It pushed everything else out of his mind—all consideration of other and possibly more feasible methods of pushing his suit. He came of a race of men who had dared and dominated, who had loved and fought, but had never learned how to work or to endure.

When he gave himself up to his dream he was almost elated, but when he came to contemplate his actual circumstances, he fell into depths of discouragement and melancholy. His uncle stood like a rock between him and his desire. He thought of trying to borrow a few thousand dollars from old Diego, and of leaving the future to luck, but he was too intelligent long to entertain such a scheme. The Don would likely have provided him with the money, and he would have done it by hypothecating more of the Delcasar lands to MacDougall. Then Ramon would have had to borrow more, and so on, until the lands upon which all his hopes and dreams were based had passed forever out of his reach.

The thing seemed hopeless, for Don Diego might well live for many years. And yet Ramon did not give up hope. He was worried, desperate and bitter, but not beaten. He had still that illogical faith in his own destiny which is the gift that makes men of action.

At this time he heard particularly disquieting

things about his uncle. Don Diego was reputed to be spending unusually large sums of money. As he generally had not much ready cash, this must mean either that he had sold land or that he had borrowed from MacDougall, in which case the land had doubtless been given as security. Once it was converted into cash in the hands of Diego, Ramon knew that his prospective fortune would swiftly vanish. He determined to watch the old man closely.

He learned that Don Diego was playing poker every night in the back room of the White Camel pool hall. Gambling was supposed to be prohibited in the town, but this sanctum was regularly the scene for a game, which had the reputation of causing more money to change hands than any other in the southwest. Ramon hung about the White Camel evening after evening, trying to learn how much his uncle was losing. He would have liked to go and stand behind his chair and watch the game, but both etiquette and pride prevented him doing this. On two nights his uncle came out surrounded by a laughing crowd, a little bit tipsy, and was hurried into a cab. Ramon had no chance to speak either to him or to any one else who had been in the game, But the third night he came out alone, heavy with liquor, talking to himself. The other players had already gone out, laughing. The place was nearly

deserted. The Don suddenly caught sight of
Ramon and came to him, laying heavy hands on
his shoulders, looking at him with bleary, tear-
filled eyes.

"My boy, my nephew," he exclaimed in Spanish,
his voice shaking with boozy emotion, "I am glad
you are here. Come I must talk to you." And
steadied by Ramon he led the way to a bench in a
corner. Here his manner suddenly changed. He
threw back his head haughtily and slapped his
knee.

"I have lost five hundred dollars tonight," he
announced proudly. "What do I care? I am a
rich man. I have lost a thousand dollars in the
last three nights. That is nothing. I am rich."

He thumped his chest, looking around defiantly.
Then he leaned forward in a confidential manner
and lowered his voice.

"But these gringos—they have gone away and
left me. You saw them? *Cabrones!* They
have got my money. That is all they want.
My boy, all gringos are alike. They want
nothing but money. They can hear the rattle of
a *peso* as far as a *burro* can smell a bear. They
are mean, stingy! Ah, my boy! It is not now as
it was in the old days. Then money counted for
nothing! Then a man could throw away his last
dollar and there were always friends to give him
more. But now your dollars are your only true

[81]

friends, and when you have lost them, you are alone indeed. Ah, my boy! The old days were the best!" The old Don bent his head over his hands and wept.

Ramon looked at him with a mighty disgust and with a resentment that filled his throat and made his head hot. He had never before realized how much broken by age and drink his uncle was. Before, he had suspected and feared that Don Diego was wasting his property; now he knew it.

The Don presently looked up again with tear-filled eyes, and went on talking, holding Ramon by the lapel of the coat in a heavy tremulous grip. He talked for almost an hour, his senile mind wandering aimlessly through the scenes of his long and picturesque career. He would tell tales of his loves and battles of fifty years ago—tales full of lust and greed and excitement. He would come back to his immediate troubles and curse the gringos again for a pack of miserable dollar-mongers, who knew not the meaning of friendship. And again his mind would leap back irrelevantly to some woman he had loved or some man he had killed in the spacious days where his imagination dwelt. Ramon listened eagerly, hoping to learn something definite about the Don's dealings with MacDougall, but the old man never touched upon this. He did tell one story to which Ramon listened with interest. He told how, twenty-five years before, he and another man named Cristobal Archulera had found a silver mine in the Guadelupe Mountains, and how he had cheated the other out of his interest by filing the claim in his own name. He told this as a capital joke, laughing and thumping his knee.

"Do you know where Archulera is now?" Ramon ventured to ask.

"Archulera? No, No; I have not seen Archulera for twenty years. I heard that he married a very common woman, half Indian. . . . I don't know what became of him."

The last of the pool players had now gone out; a Mexican boy had begun to sweep the floor; the place was about to close for the night. Ramon got his uncle to his feet with some difficulty, and led him outdoors where he looked about in vain for one of the cheap autos that served the town as taxicabs. There were only three or four of them, and none of these were in sight. The flat-wheeled street car had made its last screeching trip for the night. There was nothing for it but to take the Don by the arm and pilot him slowly homeward.

Refreshed by the night air, the old man partially sobered, walked with a steady step, and talked more eloquently and profusely than ever. Women were his subject now, and it was a subject upon which he had great store of material. He

[83]

told of the women of the South, of Sonora and Chihuahua where he had spent much of his youth, of how beautiful they were. He told of a slim little creature fifteen years old with big black eyes whom he had bought from her *peon* father, and of how she had feared him and how he had conquered her and her fear. He told of slave girls he had bought from the Navajos as children and raised for his pleasure. He told of a French woman he had loved in Mexico City and how he had fought a duel with her husband. He rose to heights of sentimentality and delved into depths of obscenity, now speaking magniloquently of his heart and what it had suffered, and again leering and chuckling like a satyr over some tale of splendid desire.

Ramon, walking silent and outwardly respectful by his side, listened to all this with a strange mixture of envy and rage. He envied the old Don the rich share he had taken of life's feast. Whatever else he might be the Don was not one of those who desire but do not dare. He had taken what he wanted. He had tasted many emotions and known the most poignant delights. And now that he was old and his blood was slow, he stood in the way of others who desired as greatly and were as avid of life as ever he had been. Ramon felt a great bitterness that clutched at his throat and half blinded his eyes. He too loved and desired. And how much more greatly he desired than ever had this old man by his side, with his wealth and his easy satisfactions! The old Don apparently had never been thwarted, and therefore he did not know how keen and punishing a blade desire may be!

Tense between the two was the enmity that ever sunders age and youth—age seeking to keep its sovereignty of life by inculcating blind respect and reverence, and youth rebellious, demanding its own with the passion of hot blood and untried flesh.

Between Old Town and New Town flowed an irrigating ditch, which the connecting street crossed by means of an old wooden bridge. The ditch was this night full of swift water, which tore at the button willows on the bank and gurgled against the bridge timbers. As they crossed it the idea came into Ramon's head that if a man were pushed into the brown water he would be swiftly carried under the bridge and drowned.

CHAPTER XI

The following Saturday evening Ramon was again riding across the *mesa,* clad in his dirty hunting clothes, with his shotgun hung in the cinches of his saddle. At the start he had been undecided where he was going. Tormented by desire and bitter over the poverty which stood between him and fulfilment, he had flung the saddle on his mare and ridden away, feeling none of the old interest in the mountains, but impelled by a great need to escape the town with all its cruel spurs and resistances.

Already the rhythm of his pony's lope and the steady beat of the breeze in his face had calmed and refreshed him. The bitter, exhausting thoughts that had been plucking at his mind gave way to the idle procession of sensations, as they tend always to do when a man escapes the artificial existence of towns into the natural, animal one of the outdoors. He began to respond to the deep appeal which the road, the sense of going somewhere, always had for him. For he came of a race of wanderers. His forbears had been restless men to cross an ocean and most of a continent in search of homes. He was bred to a life of wandering and adventure. Long pent-up days in town always made him restless, and the feel of a horse under him and of distance to be overcome never failed to give him a sense of well-being.

Crossing a little *arroyo,* he saw a covey of the blue desert quail with their white crests erect, darting among the rocks and cactus on the hill-side. It was still the close season, but he never thought of that. In an instant he was all hunter, like a good dog in sight of game. He slipped from his horse, letting the reins fall to the ground, and went running up the rocky slope, cleverly using every bit of cover until he came within range. At the first shot he killed three of the birds, and got another as they rose and whirred over the hill top. He gathered them up quickly, stepping on the head of a wounded one, and stuffed them into his pockets. He was grinning, now, and happy. The bit of excitement had washed from his mind for the time being the last vestige of worry. He lit a cigarette and lay on his back to smoke it, stretching out his legs luxuriously, watching the serene gyrations of a buzzard. When he had extracted the last possible puff from the tobacco, he went back to his horse and rode on toward Archulera's ranch, feeling a keen interest in the coarse but substantial supper which he knew the old man would give him.

His visit this time proceeded just as had all of the others, and he had never enjoyed one more thoroughly. Again the old man killed a fatted kid in his honour, and again they had a great feast of fresh brains and tripe and biscuits and coffee, with the birds, fried in deep lard, as an added luxury. Catalina served them in silence as usual, but stole now and then a quick reproachful look at Ramon. Afterward, when the girl had gone, there were many cigarettes and much talk, as before, Archulera telling over again the brave wild record of his youth. And, as always, he told, just as though he had never told it before, the story of how Diego Delcasar had cheated him out of his interest in a silver mine in the Guadelupe Mountains. As with each former telling he became this time more unrestrained in his denunciation of the man who had betrayed him.

"You are not like him," he assured Ramon with passionate earnestness. "You are generous, honourable! When your uncle is dead—when he is dead, I say—you will pay me the five thousand dollars which your family owes to mine. Am I right, *amigo?*"

Ramon, who was listening with only half an ear, was about to make some off-hand reply, as he had always done before. But suddenly a strange, stirring idea flashed through his brain. Could it be? Could that be what Archulera meant? He glanced at the man. Archulera was watching him with bright black eyes—cunning, feral—the eyes of a primitive fighting man, eyes that had never flinched at dealing death.

Ramon knew suddenly that his idea was right. Blood pounded in his temples and a red mist of excitement swam before his eyes.

"Yes!" he exclaimed, leaping to his feet. "Yes! When my uncle is dead I will pay you the five thousand dollars which the estate owes you!"

The old man studied him, showing no trace of excitement save for the brightness of his eyes.

"You swear this?" he demanded.

Ramon stood tall, his head lifted, his eyes bright.

"Yes; I swear it," he replied, more quietly now. "I swear it on my honour as a Delcasar!"

CHAPTER XII

The murder of Don Diego Delcasar, which occurred about three weeks later, provided the town with an excitement which it thoroughly enjoyed. Although there was really not a great deal to be said about the affair, since it remained from the first a complete mystery, the local papers devoted a great deal of space to it. The *Evening Journal* announced the event in a great black headline which ran all the way across the top of the first page. The right-hand column was devoted to a detailed description of the scene of the crime, while the rest of the page was occupied by a picture of the Don, by a hastily written and highly inaccurate account of his career, and by statements from prominent citizens concerning the great loss which the state had suffered in the death of this, one of its oldest and most valued citizens.

In the editorial columns the Don was described as a Spanish gentleman of the old school, and one who had always lived up to its highest traditions. The fact was especially emphasized that he had commanded the respect and confidence of both the races which made up the population of the state, and his long and honourable association in a business enterprise with a leading local attorney was cited as proof of the fact that he had been above all race antagonisms.

The morning *Herald* took a slightly different tack. Its editorial writer was a former New York newspaperman of unusual abilities who had been driven to the Southwest by tuberculosis. In an editorial which was deplored by many prominent business men, he pointed out that unpunished murderers were all too common in the State. He cited several cases like this of Don Delcasar in which prominent men had been assassinated, and no arrest had followed. Thus, only a few years before, Col. ·Manuel Escudero had been killed by a shot fired through the window of a saloon, and still more recently Don Solomon Estrella had been found drowned in a vat of sheep-dip on his own ranch. He cited statistics to show that the percentage of convictions in murder trials in that State was exceedingly small. Daringly, he asked how the citizens could expect to attract to the State the capital so much needed for its development, when assassination for personal and political purposes was there tolerated much as it had been in Europe during the Middle Ages. He ended by a plea that the Mounted

Police should be strengthened, so that it would be capable of coping with the situation.

This editorial started a controversy between the two papers which ultimately quite eclipsed in interest the fact that Don Delcasar was dead. The *Morning Journal* declared that the *Herald* editorial was in effect a covert attack upon the Mexican people, pointing out that all the cases cited were those of Mexicans, and it came gallantly and for political reason to the defence of the race. At this point the "*Tribuna del Pueblo*" of Old Town jumped into the fight with an editorial in which it was asserted that both the gringo papers were maligning the Mexican people. It pointed out that the gringos controlled the political machinery of the State, and that if murder was there tolerated the dominant race was to blame.

Meanwhile the known facts about the murder of Don Delcasar remained few, simple and unilluminating. About once a month the Don used to drive in his automobile to his lands in the northern part of the State. He always took the road across the *mesa*, which passed near the mouth of Domingo Canyon and through the scissors pass, and he nearly always went alone.

When he was half way across the *mesa*, the front tires of the Don's car had been punctured by nails driven through a board and hidden in the sand of the road. Evidently the Don had

risen to alight and investigate when he had been
shot, for his body had been found hanging across
the wind-shield of the car with a bullet hole
through the head.

The discovery of the body had been made by a
Mexican woodcutter who was on the way to town
with a load of wood. He had of course been
held by the police and had been closely questioned,
but it was easily established that he had no con-
nection with the crime.

It was evident that the Don had been shot
from ambush with a rifle, and probably from a
considerable distance, but absolutely no trace of
the assassin had been found. Not only the chief
of police and several patrolmen, and the sheriff
with a posse, but also many private citizens in
automobiles had rushed to the scene of the crime
and joined in the search. The surrounding
country was dry and rocky. Not even a track
had been found.

The motive of the murder was evidently not
robbery, for nothing had been taken, although
the Don carried a valuable watch and a considerable sum of money. Indeed, there was no evidence that the murderer had even approached the
body.

The Don had been a staunch Republican,
and the *Morning Herald,* also Republican, advanced the theory that he had been killed by

political enemies. This theory was ridiculed by the *Evening Journal,* which was Democratic.

The local police arrested as a suspect a man who was found in hiding near a water tank at the railroad station, but no evidence against him could be found and he had to be released. The sheriff extracted a confession of guilt from a sheep herder who was found about ten miles from the scene of the crime, but it was subsequently proved by this man's relatives that he was at home and asleep at the time the crime was committed, and that he was well known to be of unsound mind. For some days the newspapers continued daily to record the fact that a "diligent search" for the murderer was being conducted, but this search gradually came to an end along with public interest in the crime.

CHAPTER XIII

The day after the news of his uncle's murder reached him, Ramon lay on his bed in his darkened room fully dressed in a new suit of black. He was not ill, and anything would have been easier for him than to lie there with nothing to do but to think and to stare at a single narrow sunbeam which came through a rent in the window blind. But it was a Mexican custom, old and revered, for the family of one recently dead to lie upon its beds in the dark and so to receive the condolences of friends and the consolations of religion. To disregard this custom would have been most unwise for an ambitious young man, and besides, Ramon's mother clung tenaciously to the traditional Mexican ways, and she would not have tolerated any breach of them. At this moment she and her two daughters were likewise lying in their rooms, clad in new black silk and surrounded by other sorrowing females.

It was so still in the room that Ramon could hear the buzz of a fly in the vicinity of the solitary sunbeam, but from other parts of the house came occasional human sounds. One of these was an intermittent howling and wailing from the *placita*. This he knew was the work of two old Mexican women who made their livings by acting as professional mourners. They did not wait for an invitation but hung about like buzzards wherever there was a Mexican corpse. Seated on the ground with their black shawls pulled over their heads, they wailed with astonishing endurance until the coffin was carried from the house, when they were sure of receiving a substantial gift from the grateful relatives. Ramon resolved that he would give them ten dollars each. He felt sure they had never gotten so much. He was determined to do handsomely in all things connected with the funeral.

He could also hear faintly a rattle of wagons, foot steps and low human voices coming from the front of the house. A peep had shown him that already a line of wagons, carriages and buggies half a block long had formed in the street, and he could hear the arrival of another one every few minutes. These vehicles brought the numerous and poor relations of Don Delcasar who lived in the country. All of them would be there by night. Each one of them would come into Ramon's room and sit by his bedside and take his hand and express sympathy. Some of them would weep and some would groan, although all of them, like himself, were profoundly glad that the Don was dead. Ramon hoped that they would make their expressions brief. And later, he knew, all would gather in the room where the casket rested on two chairs. They would sit in a silent solemn circle about the room, drinking coffee and wine all night. And he would be among them, trying with all his might to look properly sad and to keep his eyes open.

All the time that he lay there in enforced idleness he was longing for action, his imagination straining forward. At last his chance had come —his chance to have her. And he would have her. He felt sure of it. He was now a rich man. As soon as the will had been read and he had come into his own, he would buy a big automobile. He would go to her, he would sweep away her doubts and hesitations. He would carry her away and marry her. She would be his.... He closed his eyes and drew his breath in sharply....

But no; he would have to wait... a decent interval. And the five thousand dollars must be gotten to Archulera. That was obviously important. And there might not be much cash. The Don had never had much ready money. He might have to sell land or sheep first. All of these things to be done, and here he lay, staring at the ceiling and listening to the wailing of old women!

There was a knock on the door.

"Entra!" he called.

The door opened softly and a tall, black-robed figure was silhouetted for a moment against the daylight before the door closed again. The black figure crossed the room and sat down by the bed, silent save for a faint rustle.

Although he could not see the face, Ramon knew that this was the priest, Father Lugaria. He knew that Father Lugaria had come to arrange for the mass over the body of Don Delcasar. He disliked Father Lugaria, and knew that the Father disliked him. This mutual antipathy was due to the fact that Ramon seldom went to Church.

There were others of his generation who showed the same indifference toward religion, and this defection of youth was a thing which the Priests bitterly contested. Ramon was perfectly willing to make a polite compromise with them. If Father Lugaria had been satisfied with an occasional appearance at early mass, a perfunctory confession now and then, the two might have been friends. But the Priest made Ramon a special object of his attention. He continually went to the Dona Delcasar with complaints and that devout woman incessantly nagged her son, holding before him always pictures of the damnation he was courting. Once in a while she even produced in him a faint twinge of fear—a recrudescence of the deep religious feeling in which he was bred —but the feeling was evanescent. The chief result of these labours on behalf of his soul had been to turn him strongly against the priest who instigated them.

Father Lugaria seemed all kindness and sympathy now. He sat close beside Ramon and took his hand. Ramon could smell the good wine on the man's breath, and could see faintly the brightness of his eyes. The grip of the priest's hand was strong, moist and surprisingly cold. He began to talk in the low monotonous voice of one accustomed to much chanting, and this droning seemed to have some hypnotic quality. It seemed to lull Ramon's mind so that he could not think what he was going to say or do.

The priest expressed his sympathy. He spoke of the great and good man the Don had been. Slowly, adroitly, he approached the real question at issue, which was how much Ramon would pay for a mass. The more he paid, the longer the mass would be, and the longer the mass the speedier would be the journey of the Don's soul through purgatory and into Paradise.

"O, my little brother in Christ!" droned the priest in his vibrant sing-song, "I must not let you

[99]

neglect this last, this greatest of things which you can do for the uncle you loved. It is unthinkable of course that his soul should go to hell—hell, where a thousand demons torture the soul for an eternity. Hell is for those who commit the worst of sins, sins they dare not lay before God for his forgiveness, secret and terrible sins— sins like murder. But few of us go through life untouched by sin. The soul must be purified before it can enter the presence of its maker.... Doubtless the soul of your uncle is in purgatory, and to you is given the sweet power to speed that soul on its upward way....

"Don Delcasar, we all know, killed.... More than once, doubtless, he took the life of a fellow man. But he did it in combat as a soldier, as a servant of the State.... That is not murder. That would not doom him to hell, which is the special punishment of secret and unforgiven murder.... But the soul of the Don must be cleansed of these earthly stains. . . ."

The strong, cold grip of the priest held Ramon with increasing power. The monotonous, hypnotic voice went on and on, becoming ever more eloquent and confident. Father Lugaria was a man of imagination, and the special home of his imagination was hell. For thirty years he had held despotic sway over the poor Mexicans who made up most of his flock, and had gathered much money for the Church, by painting word-pictures of hell. He was a veritable artist of hell. He loved hell. Again and again he digressed from the strict line of his argument to speak of hell. With all the vividness of a thing seen, he described its flames, its fiends, the terrible stink of burning flesh and the vast chorus of agony that filled it.... And for some obscure reason or purpose he always spoke of hell as the special punishment of murderers. Again and again in his discourse he coupled murder and hell.

Ramon was wearied by strong emotions and a shortness of sleep. His nerves were overstrung. This ceaseless iteration of hell and murder, murder and hell would drive him crazy, he thought. He wished mightily that the priest would have done and name his price and go. What was the sense and purpose of this endless babble about hell and murder? . . . A sickening thought struck him like a blow, leaving him weak. What if old Archulera had confessed to the priest?

Well; what if he had? A priest could not testify about what he had heard in confessional. But a priest might tell some one else.... O, God! If the man would only go and leave him to think. Hell and murder, murder and hell. The two words beat upon his brain without mercy. He longed to interrupt the priest and beg him to leave off. But for some reason he could not. He could not even turn his head and look at the man. The priest was but a clammy grip that held him and a disembodied voice that spoke of hell and murder. Had he done murder? And was there a hell? He had long ceased to believe in hell, but hell had been real to him as a child. His mother and his nurse had filled him with the fear of hell. He had been bred in the fear of hell. It was in his flesh and bones if not in his mind, and the priest had hypnotized his mind. Hell was real to him again. Fear of hell came up from the past which vanishes but is never gone, and gripped him like a great ugly monster. It squeezed a cold sweat out of his body and made his skin prickle and his breath come short. . . .

The priest dropped the subject of hell, and spoke again of the mass. He mentioned a sum of money. Ramon nodded his head muttering his assent like a sick man. The grip on his hand relaxed.

"Good-bye, my little brother," murmured the priest. "May Christ be always with you." His gown rustled across the room and as he opened the door, Ramon saw his face for a moment—a sallow, shrewd face, bedewed with the sweat of a great effort, but wearing a smile of triumphant satisfaction.

Ramon lay sick and exhausted. It seemed to

him that there was no air in the room. He was suffocating. His body burned and prickled. He rose and tore loose his collar. He must get out of this place, must have air and movement.

It was dusk now. The wailing of the old women had ceased. Doubtless they were being rewarded with supper. He began stripping off his clothes—his white shirt and his new suit of black. Eagerly rummaging in the closet he found his old clothes, which he wore on his trips to the mountains.

In the dim light he slipped out of the house, indistinguishable from any Mexican boy that might have been about the place. He saddled the little mare in the corral, mounted and galloped away—through Old Town, where skinny dogs roamed in dark narrow streets and men and women sat and smoked in black doorways—and out upon the valley road. There he spurred his mare without mercy, and they flew over the soft dust. The rush of the air in his face, and the thud and quiver of living flesh under him were infinitely sweet.

He stopped at last five miles from town on the bank of the river. It was a swift muddy river, wandering about in a flood plain a quarter of a mile wide, and at this point chewing noisily at a low bank forested with scrubby cottonwoods.

Dismounting, he stripped and plunged into the

river. It was only three feet deep, but he wallowed about in it luxuriously, finding great comfort in the caress of the cool water, and of the soft fine sand upon the bottom which clung about his toes and tickled the soles of his feet. Then he climbed out on the bank and stood where the breeze struck him, rubbing the water off of his slim strong body with the flats of his hands.

When he had put on his clothes, he indulged his love of lying flat on the ground, puffing a cigarette and blowing smoke at the first stars. A hunting owl flitted over his head on muffled wing; a coyote yapped in the bushes; high up in the darkness he heard the whistle of pinions as a flock of early ducks went by.

He took the air deeply into his lungs and stretched out his legs. In this place fear of hell departed from his mind as some strong liquors evaporate when exposed to the open air. The splendid healthy animal in him was again dominant, and it could scarcely conceive of death and had nothing more to do with hell than had the owl and the coyote that killed to live. Here he felt at peace with the earth beneath him and the sky above. But one thought came to disturb him and it was also sweet—the thought of a woman, her eyes full of promise, the curve of her mouth. . . . She was waiting for him, she would be his. That was real. . . . Hell was a dream.

He saw now the folly of his fears about Archulera, too. Archulera never went to church. There was no danger that he would ever confess to any one. And even if he did, he could scarcely injure Ramon. For Ramon had done no wrong. He had but promised an old man his due, righted an ancient wrong.... He smiled.

Slowly he mounted and rode home, filled with thoughts of the girl, to put on his mourning clothes and take his decorous place in the circle that watched his uncle's bier.

CHAPTER XIV

All the ceremonies and procedures, religious and legal, which had been made necessary by the death of Don Diego Delcasar, were done. The body of the Don had been taken to the church in Old Town and placed before the altar, the casket covered with black cloth and surrounded by candles in tall silver candlesticks which stood upon the floor. A Mass of impressive length had been spoken over it by Father Lugaria assisted by numerous priests and altar boys, and at the end of the ceremony the hundreds of friends and relatives of the Don, who filled the church, had lifted up their voices in one of the loudest and most prolonged choruses of wailing ever heard in that country, where wailing at a funeral is as much a matter of formal custom as is cheering at a political convention. Afterwards a cortege nearly a mile in length, headed by a long string of carriages and tailed by a crowd of poor Mexicans trudging hatless in the dust, had made the hot and wearisome journey to the cemetery in the sandhills.

Then the will had been read and had revealed that Ramon Delcasar was heir to the bulk of his uncle's estate, and that he was thereby placed in possession of money, lands and sheep to the value of about two hundred thousand dollars. It was said by those who knew that the Don's estate had once been at least twice that large, and there were some who irreverently remarked that he had been taken off none too soon for the best interests of his heirs.

Shortly after the reading of the will, Ramon rode to the Archulera ranch, starting before daylight and returning after dark. He exchanged greetings with the old man, just as he had always done.

"Accept my sympathy, *amigo*," Archulera said in his formal, polite way, "that you have lost your uncle, the head of your great family."

"I thank you, friend," Ramon replied. "A man must bear these things. Here is something I promised you," he added, laying a small heavy canvas bag upon the table, just as he had always laid a package of tobacco or some other small gift.

Old Archulera nodded without looking at the bag.

"Thank you," he said.

Afterward they talked about the bean crop and the weather, and had an excellent dinner of goat meat cooked with chile.

In town Ramon found himself a person of no-

ticeably increased importance. One of his first
acts had been to buy a car, and he had attracted
much attention while driving this about the
streets, learning to manipulate it. He killed one
chicken and two dogs and handsomely reimbursed
their owners. These minor accidents were due
to his tendency, the result of many years of horse-
manship, to throw his weight back on the steering
wheel and shout "whoa!" whenever a sudden emer-
gency occurred. But he was apt, and soon was
running his car like an expert.

His personal appearance underwent a change
too. He had long cherished a barbaric leaning
toward finery, which lack of money had prevented
him from indulging. Large diamonds fascinated
him, and a leopard skin vest was a thing he had
always wanted to own. But these weaknesses he
now rigorously suppressed. Instead he noted
carefully the dress of Gordon Roth and of other
easterners whom he saw about the hotel, and
ordered from the best local tailor a suit of quiet
colour and conservative cut, but of the very best
English material. He bought no jewelry except a
single small pearl for his necktie. His hat, his
shoes, the way he had his neck shaved, all were
changed as the result of a painstaking observation
such as he had never practised before. He
wanted to make himself as much as possible like
the men of Julia's kind and class. And this desire

modified his manner and speech as well as his appearance. He was careful, always watching himself. His manner was more reserved and quiet than ever, and this made him appear older and more serious. He smiled when he overheard a woman say that "he took the death of his uncle much harder than she would have expected."

Ramon now received business propositions every day. Men tried to sell him all sorts of things, from an idea to a ranch, and most of them seemed to proceed on the assumption that, being young and newly come into his money, he should part with it easily. Several of the opportunities offered him had to do with the separation of the poor Mexicans from their land holdings. A prominent attorney came all the way from a town in the northern part of the State to lay before him a proposition of this kind. This lawyer, named Cooley, explained that by opening a store in a certain rich section of valley land, opportunities could be created for lending the Mexicans money. Whenever there was a birth, a funeral or a marriage among them, the Mexicans needed money, and could be persuaded to sign mortgages, which they generally could not read. In each Mexican family there would be either a birth, a marriage or a death once in three years on an average. Three such events would enable the lender to gain possession of a ranch. And Cooley had an eastern client who would then buy the land at a good figure. It was a chance for Ramon to double his money.

"You've got the money and you know the native people," Cooley argued earnestly. "I've got the sucker and I know the law. It's a sure thing."

Ramon thanked him politely and refused firmly. The idea of robbing a poor Mexican of his ranch by nine years of usury did not appeal to him at all. In the first place, it would be a long, slow tedious job, and besides, poor people always aroused his pity, just as rich ones stirred his greed and envy. He was predatory, but lion-like, he scorned to spring on small game. He did not realize that a lion often starves where a jackal grows fat.

Only one opportunity came to him which interested him strongly. A young Irishman named Hurley explained to him that it was possible to buy mules in Mexico, where a revolution was going on, for ten dollars each at considerable personal risk, to run them across the Rio Grande and to sell them to the United States army for twenty dollars. Here was a gambler's chance, action and adventure. It caught his fancy and tempted him. But he had no thought of yielding. Another purpose engrossed him.

These weeks after his uncle's funeral gave him his first real grapple with the world of business, and the experience tended to strengthen him in a certain cynical self-assurance which had been growing in him ever since he first went away to college, and had met its first test in action when he spoke the words that lead to the Don's death. He felt a deep contempt for most of these men who came to him with their schemes and their wares. He saw that most of them were ready enough to swindle him, though few of them would have had the courage to rob him with a gun. Probably not one of them would have dared to kill a man for money, but they were ready enough to cheat a poor *pelado* out of his living, which often came to the same thing. He felt that he was bigger than most of them, if not better. His self-respect was strengthened.

"Life is a fight," he told himself, feeling that he had hit upon a profound and original idea. "Every man wants pretty women and money. He gets them if he has enough nerve and enough sense. And somebody else gets hurt, because there aren't enough pretty women and money to go around."

It seemed to him that this was the essence of all wisdom.

CHAPTER XV

Ramon had always been rather a solitary figure in his own town. Although he belonged nominally to the "bunch" of young gringos, Jews and Mexicans, who foregathered at the White Camel Pool Hall, their amusements did not hold his interest very strongly. They played a picayune game of poker, which resulted in a tangled mass of debt; they went on occasional mild sprees, and on Saturday nights they visted the town's red light district, hardy survivor of several vice crusades, where they danced with portly magdalenes in gaudy kimonos to the music of a mechanical piano, luxuriating in conscious wickedness.

All of this had seemed romantic and delightfully vicious to Ramon a few years before, but it soon palled on his restless and discontented spirit. He had formed the habit of hunting alone, and had found adventures more to his taste. But now he found himself in company more than ever before. He was bid to every frolic that took place. In the White Camel he was often the centre of a small group, which included men older than himself who had never paid any attention to him before, but now addressed him with a certain deference. Although he understood well enough that most of the attentions paid him had an interested motive, he enjoyed the sense of leadership which these gatherings gave him. If he was not a real leader now, he intended to become one. He listened to what men said, watched them, and said little himself. He was quick to grasp the fact that a reputation for shrewdness and wisdom is made by the simple method of keeping the mouth shut.

He made many acquaintances among the new element which had recently come to town from the East in search of health or money, but he made no real friends because none of these men inspired him with respect. Only one man he attached to himself, and that one by the simple tie of money. His name was Antonio Cortez. He was a small, skinny, sallow Mexican with a great moustache, behind which he seemed to be discreetly hiding, and a consciously cunning eye. Of an old and once wealthy Spanish family, he had lost all of his money by reason of a lack of aptitude for business, and made his living as a sort of professional political henchman. He was a bearer of secret messages, a maker of deals, an eavesdropper. The Latin aptitude for intrigue he had in a high degree. He was capable of almost anything in

[113]

the way of falsehood or evasion, but he had that great capacity for loyalty which is so often the virtue of weaklings.

"I have known your family for many years," he told Ramon importantly, "And I feel an interest in you, almost as though you were my own son. You need an older friend to advise you, to attend to details in the management of your great estate. You will probably go into politics and you need a political manager. As an old friend of your family I want to do these things for you. What do you say?"

Ramon answered without any hesitation and prompted solely by intuition:

"I thank you, friend, and I accept your offer."

He knew instinctively that he could trust this man and also dominate him. It was just such a follower that he needed. Nothing was said about money, but on the first of the month Ramon mailed Cortez a check for a hundred dollars, and that became his regular salary.

CHAPTER XVI

About two weeks after the Don's funeral, Ramon received a summons which he had been vaguely expecting. He was asked by Mr. Mac-Dougall's secretary over the telephone to call, whenever it would be convenient, at Mr. Mac-Dougall's office.

He knew just what this meant. MacDougall would try to make with him an arrangement somewhat similar to the one he had had with the Don. Ramon knew that he did not want such an arrangement on any terms. He felt confident that no one could swindle him, but at the same time he was half afraid of the Scotchman; he felt instinctively that MacDougall was a man for him to avoid. And besides, he intended to use his lands in his own way. He would sell part of them to the railroad, which was projected to be built through them, if he could get a good price; but the hunger for owning land, for dominating a part of the earth, was as much a part of him as his right hand. He wanted no modern business partnership. He wanted to be *"el patron,"* as so many Delcasars had been before him.

Here was a temptation to be dramatic, to hurl

a picturesque defiance at the gringo. Ramon might have yielded to it a few months before. Sundry brave speeches flashed through his mind, as it was. But he resolutely put them aside. There was too much at stake ... his love. He determined to call on MacDougall promptly and to be polite.

MacDougall was a heavy, bald man of Scotch descent, and very true to type. He had come to town from the East about fifteen years before with his wife and his two tall, raw-boned children —a boy and a girl. The family had been very poor. They had lived in a small *adobe* house on the *mesa.* For ten years Mrs. Mac-Dougall had done all of her own housework, including the washing; the two children had gone to school in clothes that seemed always too small for them; and MacDougall had laboured obscurely day and night in a small dark office. During these ten years the MacDougalls had been completely overlooked by local society, and if they felt any resentment they did not show it.

Meantime MacDougall had been systematic-ally and laboriously laying the foundations of a fortune. His passion was for land. He loaned money on land, chiefly to Mexicans, and he took mortgages on land in return for defending his Mexican clients, largely on criminal charges. Some of the land he farmed, and some he rented, but much of it lay idle, and the taxes he had to pay kept his family poor long after it might have been comfortable. But his lands rose steadily in value; he began selling, discreetly; and the Mac-Dougalls came magnificently into their own. MacDougall was now one of the wealthiest men in the State. In five years his way of living had undergone a great change. He owned a large brick house in the highlands and had several servants. The boy had gone to Harvard, and the girl to Vassar. Neither of them was so gawky now, and both of them were much sought socially during their vacations at home. MacDougall himself had undergone a marked change for a man past fifty. He had become a stylish dresser and looked younger. He drove to work in a large car with a chauffeur. In the early morning he went riding on the *mesa,* mounted on a big Kentucky fox-trotter, clad in English riding clothes, jouncing solemnly up and down on his flat saddle, and followed by a couple of carefully-laundered white poodles. On these expeditions he was a source of great edification and some amusement to the natives.

In the town he was a man of weight and influence, but the country Mexicans hated him. Once when he was looking over some lands recently acquired by the foreclosure of mortgages, a bullet had whistled close to his ear, and another had punctured the hood of his car. He now hired a man to do his "outside work."

Thus both MacDougall and his children had thrived and developed on their wealth. Mrs. MacDougall, perhaps, had been the sacrifice. She remained a tall, thin, pale, tired-looking woman with large hands that were a record of toil. She laboured at her new social duties and "pleasures" in exactly the same spirit that she had formerly laboured at the wash tub.

MacDougall's offices now occupied all of the ground floor of a large new building which he had built. Like everything else of his authorship this building represented a determined effort to lend the town an air of Eastern elegance. It was finished in an imitation of white marble and the offices had large plate glass windows which bore in gilt letters the legend: "MacDougall Land and Cattle Company, Inc." Within, half a dozen girls in glass cages could be seen working at typewriters and adding machines, while a cashier occupied a little office of his own with a large safe at his back, a little brass grating in front of him, and a revolver visible not far from his right hand.

The creator of this magnificence sat behind a glasstop desk at the far end of a large and sunny office with a bare and slippery floor. Many a Mexican beggar for mercy, with a mortgage on his home, had walked across this forbidding expanse of polished hardwood toward the big man with the merciless eye, as fearfully as ever a *peon*, sentenced to forty lashes and salt in his wounds, approached the seat of his owner to plead for a whole skin. Truly, the weak can but change masters.

This morning MacDougall was all affability. As he stood up behind his desk, clad in a light grey suit, large and ruddy, radiant of health and prosperity, he was impressive, almost splendid. Only the eyes, small and closeset, revealed the worried and calculating spirit of the man.

"Mr. Delcasar," he said when they had shaken hands and sat down, "I am glad to welcome you to this office, and I hope to see you here many times more. I will not waste time, for we are both busy men. I asked you to come here because I want to suggest a sort of informal partnership between us, such as I had with your late uncle, one of my best friends. I believe my plan will be for the best interests of both of us. . . . I suppose you know about what the arrangement was between the Don and myself?"

"No; not in detail," Ramon confessed. He felt MacDougall's power at once. Facing the man was a different matter from planning an interview with him when alone. But he retained sense enough to let MacDougall do the talking.

[119]

"Have a cigar," the great man continued, full of sweetness, pushing a large and fragrant box of perfectos across the desk. "I will outline the situation to you briefly, as I see it." Nothing could have seemed more frank and friendly than his manner.

"As you doubtless know," he went on, "your estate includes a large area of mountain and *mesa* land—a little more than nine thousand acres I believe—north and west of the San Antonio River in Arriba County. I own nearly as much land on the east side of the river. The valley itself is owned by a number of natives in small farming tracts.

"I believe your estate also includes a few small parcels of land in the valley, but not enough, you understand, to be of much value by itself. Your uncle also owned a few tracts in the valley east of the river which he transferred to me, for a consideration, because they abutted upon my holdings.

"Now the valley, as I scarcely need tell you, is the key to the situation. In the first place, if the country is to be properly developed as sheep and cattle range, the valley will furnish the farming land upon which hay for winter use can be raised, and it also furnishes some good winter range. Moreover, it is now an open secret that the Denver and Rio Grande Railroad proposes building a branch line through that country and into the San Juan Valley. No surveys have been made, but it is certain that the road must follow the San Antonio to the top of the divide. There is no other way through. I became aware of this project some time ago through my eastern connections, and told your uncle about it. He and I joined forces for the purpose of gaining control of the San Antonio Valley, and of the railroad right-of-way.

"The proposition is a singularly attractive one. Not only could the right-of-way be sold for a very large sum, but we would afterward own a splendid bit of cattle range, with farming land in the valley, and with a railroad running through the centre of it. There is nothing less than a fortune to be made in the San Antonio Valley, Mr. Delcasar.

"And the lands in the valley can be acquired. Some of the small owners will sell outright. Furthermore, they are all frequently in need of money, especially during dry years when the crops are not good. By advancing loans judiciously, and taking land as security, title can often be acquired. . . . I daresay you are not wholly unfamiliar with the method.

"This work, Mr. Delcasar, requires large capital, which I can command. It also requires certain things which you have in an unusual degree. You are of Spanish descent, you speak the language fluently. You have political and family prestige among the natives. All of this will be of great service in persuading the natives to sell, and in getting the necessary information about land titles, which, as you know, requires much research in old Spanish Church records and much interviewing of the natives themselves.

"In the actual making of purchases, my name need not appear. In fact, I think it is very desirable that it should not appear. But understand that I will furnish absolutely all of the capital for the enterprise. I am offering you, Mr. Delcasar, an opportunity to make a fortune without investing a cent, and I feel that I can count upon your acceptance."

At the close of this discourse, Ramon felt like a surf-bather who has been overwhelmed by a great and sudden wave and comes up gasping for breath and struggling for a foothold. Never had he heard anything so brilliantly plausible, for never before had he come into contact with a good mind in full action. Yet he regained his balance in a moment. He was accustomed to act by intuition, not by logic, and his intuition was all against accepting MacDougall's offer. He was not deceived by the Scotchman's show of friendship and beneficence; he himself had an aptitude for pretence, and he understood it better

than he would have understood sincerity. He
knew that whether he formed this partnership or
not, there was sure to be a struggle between him
and MacDougall for the dominance of the San
Antonio Valley. And his instinct was to stand
free and fight; not to come to grips. MacDougall
was a stronger man than he. The one advantage
which he had—his influence over the natives—
he must keep in his own hands, and not let his
adversary turn it against him.

He took his cigar out of his mouth, looked at
it a moment, and cleared his throat.

"Mr. MacDougall," he said slowly, "this offer
makes me proud. That you should have so much
confidence in me as to wish to make me your partner is most gratifying. I am sorry that I must
refuse. I have other plans. . . ."

MacDougall nodded, interrupting. This was
evidently a contingency he had calculated.

"I'm sorry, Mr. Delcasar. I had hoped to be
permanently associated with you in this venture.
But I think I understand. You are young.
Perhaps marriage, a home are your immediate
objects, and you need cash at once, rather than
a somewhat distant prospect of greater wealth.
In that case I think I can meet your wishes. I
am prepared to make you a good offer for all of
your holdings in the valley, and those immediately

adjoining it. The exact amount I cannot state at this moment, but I feel sure we could agree as to price."

Ramon was taken aback by the promptness of the counter, confused, forced to think. Money was a thing he wanted badly. He had little cash. If MacDougall would give him fifty thousand, he could go with Julia anywhere. He would be free. But again the inward prompting, sure and imperative, said no. He wanted the girl above all things. But he wanted land, too. His was the large and confident greed of youth. And he could have the girl without making this concession. MacDougall wanted to take the best of his land and push him out of the game as a weakling, a negligible. He wouldn't submit. He would fight, and in his own way. What he wanted now was to end the interview, to get away from this battering, formidable opponent. He rose.

"I will think it over, Mr. MacDougall," he said. "And meantime, if you will send me an offer in writing, I will appreciate it."

Some of the affability faded from Mac-Dougall's face as he too rose, and the worried look in his little grey eyes intensified, as though he sensed the fact that this was an evasion. None-the-less he said good-bye cordially and promised to write the letter.

Ramon went back to his office, his mind stimulated, working intensely. Never before had he thought so clearly and purposefully. He got out an old government map of Arriba County, and with the aid of the deeds in the safe which contained all his uncle's important papers, he managed to mark off his holdings. The whole situation became as clear to him as a checker game. He owned a bit of land in the valley which ran all the way across it, and far out upon the *mesa* in a long narrow strip. That was the way land holdings were always divided under the Spanish law—into strips a few hundred feet wide, and sometimes as much as fourteen miles long. This strip would in all probability be vital to the proposed right-of-way. It explained MacDougall's eagerness to take him as a partner or else to buy him out. By holding it, he would hold the key to the situation.

In order really to dominate the country and to make his property grow in value he would have to own more of the valley. And he could not get money enough to buy except very slowly. But he could use his influence with the natives to prevent MacDougall from buying. MacDougall was a gringo. The Mexicans hated him. He had been shot at. Ramon could "preach the race issue," as the politicians put it.

The important thing was to strengthen and

CHAPTER XVII

He had received a note of sympathy from her soon after his uncle's death and he had called at the Roths' once, but had found several other callers there and no opportunity of being alone with her. Then she had gone away on a two-weeks automobile trip to the Mesa Verde National Park, so that he had seen practically nothing of her. But all of this time he had been thinking of her more confidently than ever before. He was rich now, he was strong. All of the preliminaries had been finished. He could go to her and claim her.

He called her on the telephone from his office, and the Mexican maid answered. She would see if Miss Roth was in. After a long wait she reported that Miss Roth was out. He tried again that day, and a third time the next morning with a like result.

This filled him with anxious, angry bewilderment. He felt sure she had not really been out all three times. Were her mother and brother keeping his message from her? Or had something turned her against him? He remembered with a keen pang of anxiety, for the first time, the insinuations of Father Lugaria. Could that miserable rumour have reached her? He had no idea how she would have taken it if it had. He really did not know or understand this girl at all; he merely loved her and desired her with a desire which had become the ruling necessity of his life. To him she was a being of a different sort, from a different world—a mystery. They had nothing in common but a rebellious discontent with life, and this glamorous bewildering thing, so much stronger than they, so far beyond their comprehension, which they called their love.

That was the one thing he knew and counted on. He knew how imperiously it drove him, and he knew that she had felt its power too. He had seen it shine in her eyes, part her lips; he had heard it in her voice, and felt it tremble in her body. If only he could get to her this potent thing would carry them to its purpose through all barriers.

Angry and resolute, he set himself to a systematic campaign of telephoning. At last she answered. Her voice was level, quiet, weary.

"But I have an engagement for tonight," she told him.

"Then let me come tomorrow," he urged.

"No; I can't do that. Mother is having some people to dinner..."

At last he begged her to set a date, but she refused, declared that her plans were unfixed, told him to call "some other time."

His touchy pride rebelled now. He cursed these gringos. He hated them. He wished for the power to leave her alone, to humble her by neglect. But he knew that he did have it. Instead he waited a few days and then drove to the house in his car, having first carefully ascertained by watching that she was at home.

All three of them received him in their sitting room, which they called the library. It was an attractive room, sunny and tastefully furnished, with a couple of book cases filled with new-looking books in sets, a silver tea service on a little wheeled table, flowers that matched the wall paper, and a heavy mahogany table strewn with a not-too-disorderly array of magazines and paper knives. It was the envy of the local women with social aspirations because it looked elegant and yet comfortable.

Conversation was slow and painful. Mrs. Roth and her son were icily formal, confining themselves to the most commonplace remarks. And Julia did not help him, as she had on his first visit. She looked pale and tired and carefully avoided his eyes.

When he had been there about half an hour, Mrs. Roth turned to her daughter.

"Julia," she said, "If we are going to get to Mrs. MacDougall's at half-past four you must go and get ready. You will excuse her, won't you Mr. Delcasar?"

The girl obediently went up stairs without shaking hands, and a few minutes later Ramon went away, feeling more of misery and less of self-confidence than ever before in his life.

He almost wholly neglected his work. Cortez brought him a report that MacDougall had a new agent, who was working actively in Arriba County, but he paid no attention to it. His life seemed to have lost purpose and interest. For the first time he doubted her love. For the first time he really feared that he would lose her.

Most of his leisure was spent riding or walking about the streets, in the hope of catching a glimpse of her. He passed her house as often as he dared, and studied her movements. When he saw her in the distance he felt an acute thrill of mingled hope and misery. Only once did he meet her fairly, walking with her brother, and then she either failed to see him or pretended not to.

One afternoon about five o'clock he left his office and started home in his car. A storm was piling up rapidly in big black clouds that rose from behind the eastern mountains like giants peering from ambush. It was sultry; there were loud peals of thunder and long crooked flashes of lightning. At this season of late summer the weather staged such a portentous display almost every afternoon, and it rained heavily in the mountains; but the showers only reached the thirsty *mesa* and valley lands about one day in four.

Ramon drove home slowly, gloomily wondering whether it would rain and hoping that it would. A Southwesterner is always hoping for rain, and in his present mood the rush and beat of a storm would have been especially welcome.

His hopes were soon fulfilled. There was a cold blast of wind, carrying a few big drops, and then a sudden, drumming downpour that tore up the dust of the street and swiftly converted it into a sea of mud cut by yellow rivulets.

As his car roared down the empty street, he glimpsed a woman standing in the shelter of a big cottonwood tree, cowering against its trunk. A quick thrill shot through his body. He jammed down the brake so suddenly that his car skidded and sloughed around. He carefully turned and brought up at the curb.

She started at sight of him as he ran across the side-walk toward her.

"Come on quick!" he commanded, taking her by the arm, "I'll get you home." Before she had time to say anything he had her in the car, and they were driving toward the Roth house.

By the time they had reached it the first strength
of the shower was spent, and there was only a
light scattering rain with a rift showing in the
clouds over the mountains.

He deliberately passed the house, putting on
more speed as he did so.

"But ... I thought you were going to take me
home," she said, putting a hand on his arm.

"I'm not," he announced, without looking
around. His hands and eyes were fully occupied
with his driving, but a great suspense held his
breath. The hand left his arm, and he heard her
settle back in her seat with a sigh. A great
warm wave of joy surged through him.

He took the mountain road, which was a short
cut between Old Town and the mountains,
seldom used except by wood wagons. Within
ten minutes they were speeding across the *mesa*.
The rain was over and the clouds running across
the sky in tatters before a fresh west wind. Before them the rolling grey-green waste of the
mesa, spotted and veined with silver waters,
reached to the blue rim of the mountains—
empty and free as an undiscovered world.

He slowed his car to ten miles an hour and
leaned back, steering with one hand. The other
fell upon hers, and closed over it. For a time
they drove along in silence, conscious only of that

electrical contact, and of the wind playing in their faces and the soft rhythmical hum of the great engine.

At the crest of a rise he stopped the car and stood up, looking all about at the vast quiet wilderness, filling his lungs with air. He liked that serene emptiness. He had always felt at peace with these still desolate lands that had been the background of most of his life. Now, with the consciousness of the woman beside him, they filled him with a sort of rapture, an ecstasy of reverence that had come down to him perhaps from savage forebears who had worshipped the Earth Mother with love and awe.

He dropped down beside her again and without hesitation gathered her into his arms. After a moment he held her a little away from him and looked into her eyes.

"Why wouldn't you let me come to see you? Why did you treat me that way?" he plead.

She dropped her eyes.

"They made me."

"But why? Because I'm a Mexican? And does that make any difference to you?"

"O, I can't tell you.... They say awful things about you. I don't believe them. No; nothing about you makes any difference to me."

He held her close again.

[133]

"Then you'll go away with me?"

"Yes," she answered slowly, nodding her head. "I'll go anywhere with you."

"Now!" he demanded. "Will you go now? We can drive through Scissors Pass to Abol on the Southeastern and take a train to Denver..."

"O, no, not now," she plead. "Please not now.... I can't go like this..."

"Yes; now," he urged. "We'll never have a better chance...."

"I beg you, if you love me, don't make me go now. I must think ... and get ready.... Why I haven't even got any powder for my nose."

They both laughed. The tension was broken. They were happy.

"Give me a little while to get ready," she proposed, "and I'll go when you say."

"You promise?"

"Cross my heart.... On my life and honour. Please take me home now, so they won't suspect anything. If only nobody sees us! Please hurry. It'll be dark pretty soon. You can write to me. It's so lonely out here!"

He turned his car and drove slowly townward, his free hand seeking hers again. It was dusk when they reached the streets. Stopping his car in the shadow of a tree, he kissed her and helped her out.

He sat still and watched her out of sight. A

tinge of sadness and regret crept into his mind, and as he drove homeward it grew into an active discontent with himself. Why had he let her go? True, he had proved her love, but now she was to be captured all over again. He ought to have taken her. He had been a fool. She would have gone. She had begged him not to take her, but if he had insisted, she would have gone. He had been a fool!

CHAPTER XVIII

The second morning after this ride, while he was labouring over a note to the girl, he was amazed to get one from her postmarked at Lorietta, a station a hundred miles north of town at the foot of the Mora Mountains, in which many of the town people spent their summer vacations. It was a small square missive, exhaling a faint scent of lavender, and was simple and direct as a telegram.

"We have gone to the Valley Ranch for a month," she wrote. "We had not intended to go until August, but there was a sudden change of plans. Somebody saw you and me yesterday. I had an awful time. Please don't try to see me or write to me while we're here. It will be best for us. I'll be back soon. I love you."

He sat glumly thinking over this letter for a long time. The disappointment of learning that he would not see her for a month was bad enough, but it was not the worst thing about this sudden development. For this made him realize what alert and active opposition he faced on the part of her mother and brother. Their dislike for him had been made manifest again and again,

[136]

but he had supposed that Julia was successfully deceiving them as to his true relations with her. He had thought that he was regarded merely as an undesirable acquaintance; but if they were changing their plans because of him, taking the girl out of his reach, they must have guessed the true state of affairs. And for all that he knew, they might leave the country at any time. His heart seemed to give a sharp twist in his body at this thought. He must take her as soon as she returned to town. He could not afford to miss another chance. And meantime his affairs must be gotten in order.

He had been neglecting his new responsibilities, and there was an astonishing number of things to be done—debts to be paid, tax assessments to be protested, men to be hired for the sheep-shearing. His uncle had left his affairs at loose ends, and on all hands were men bent on taking advantage of the fact. But he knew the law; he had known from childhood the business of raising sheep on the open range which was the backbone of his fortune; and he was held in a straight course by the determination to keep his resources together so that they would strengthen him in his purpose.

A few weeks before, he had sent Cortez to Arriba County to attend to some minor matters there, and incidentally to learn if possible what MacDougall was doing. Cortez had spent a large part of his time talking with the Mexicans in the San Antonio Valley, eavesdropping on conversations in little country stores, making friends, and asking discreet questions at *bailes* and *fiestas*.

"Well; how goes it up there?" Ramon asked him when he came to the office to make his report.

"It looks bad enough," Cortez replied lighting with evident satisfaction the big cigar his patron had given him. "MacDougall has men working there all the time. He bought a small ranch on the edge of the valley just the other day. He is not making very fast progress, but he'll own the valley in time if we don't stop him."

"But who is doing the work? Who is his agent?" Ramon enquired.

"Old Solomon Alfego, for one. He's boss of the county, you know. He hates a gringo as much as any man alive, but he loves a dollar, too, and MacDougall has bought him, I'm afraid. I think MacDougall is lending money through him, getting mortgages on ranches that way."

"Well; what do you think we had better do?" Ramon enquired. The situation looked bad on its face, but he could see that Cortez had a plan.

"Just one thing I thought of," the little man answered slowly. "We have got to get Alfego on our side. If we can do that, we can keep out MacDougall and everybody else . . . buy when we get ready. We couldn't pay Alfego much, but we could let him in on the railroad deal . . . something MacDougall won't do. And Alfego, you know, is a *penitente*. He's *hermano mayor* (chief brother) up there. And all those little *rancheros* are *penitentes*. It's the strongest *penitente* county in the State, and you know none of the *penitentes* like gringos. None of those fellows like MacDougall; they're all afraid of him. All they like is his money. You haven't so much money, but you could spend some. You could give a few *bailes*. You are Mexican; your family is well-known. If you were a *penitente*, too. . . ."

Cortez left his sentence hanging in the air. He nodded his head slowly, his cigar cocked at a knowing angle, looking at Ramon through narrowed lids.

Ramon sat looking straight before him for a moment. He saw in imagination a procession of men trudging half-naked in the raw March weather, their backs gashed so that blood ran down to their heels, beating themselves and each other. . . . The *penitentes!* Other men, even gringos, had risen to power by joining the order. Why not he? It would give him just the prestige and standing he needed in that country. He would lose a little blood. He would win . . . everything!

CHAPTER XIX

He was all ready to leave for Arriba County when one more black mischance came to bedevil him. Cortez came into the office with a worried look in his usually unrevealing eyes.

"There's a woman in town looking for you," he announced. "A Mexican girl from the country. She was asking everybody she met where to find you. You ought to be more careful. I took her to my house and promised I would bring you right away."

Cortez lived in a little square box of a brick cottage, which he had been buying slowly for the past ten years and would probably never own. In its parlour, gaudy with cheap, new furniture, Ramon confronted Catalina Archulera. She was clad in a dirty calico dress, and her shoes were covered with the dust of long tramping, as was the black shawl about her head and shoulders. Once he had thought her pretty, but now she looked to him about as attractive as a clod of earth.

She stood before him with downcast eyes, speechless with misery and embarassment. At first he was utterly puzzled as to what could have brought her there. Then with a queer mixture of anger and pity and disgust, he noticed the swollen bulk of her healthy young body.

"Catalina! Why did you come here?" he blurted, all his self-possession gone for a moment.

"My father sent me," she replied, as simply as though that were an all-sufficient explanation.

"But why did you tell him . . . it was I? Why didn't you come to me first?"

"He made me tell," Catalina rolled back her sleeve and showed some blue bruises. "He beat me," she explained without emotion.

"What did he tell you to say?"

"He told me to come to you and show you how I am. . . . That is all."

Ramon swore aloud with a break in his voice. For a long moment he stood looking at her, bewildered, disgusted. It somehow seemed to him utterly wrong, utterly unfair that this thing should have happened, and above all that it should have happened now. He had taken other girls, as had every other man, but never before had any such hard luck as this befallen him. And now, of all times!

In Catalina he felt not the faintest interest. Before him was the proof that once he had desired her. Now that desire had vanished as completely as his childhood.

And she was Archulera's daughter. That was

the hell of it! Archulera was the one man of all men whom he could least afford to offend. And he knew just how hard to appease the old man would be. For among the Mexicans, seduction is a crime which, in theory and often in practice, can be atoned only by marriage or by the shedding of blood. Marriage is the door to freedom for the women, but virginity is a thing greatly revered and carefully guarded. The unmarried girl is always watched, often locked up, and he who appropriates her to his own purpose is violating a sacred right and offending her whole family.

In the towns, all this has been somewhat changed, as the customs of any country suffer change in towns. But old Archulera, living in his lonely canyon, proud of his high lineage, would be the hardest of men to appease. And meantime, what was to be done with the girl?

It was this problem which brought his wits back to him. A plan began to form in his mind. He saw that in sending her to him Archulera had really played into his hands. The important thing now was to keep her away from her father. He looked at her again, and the pity which he always felt for weaklings welled up in him. He knew many Mexican ranches in the valley where he could keep her in comfort for a small amount. That would serve a double purpose. The old man would be kept in ignorance as to what Ramon intended, and the girl would be saved from furthur punishment. Meantime, he could send Cortez to see Archulera and find out what money would do.

The whole affair was big with potential damage to him. Some of his enemies might find out about it and make a scandal. Archulera might come around in an ugly mood and make trouble. The girl might run away and come to town again. And yet, now that he had a plan, he was all confidence.

Cortez kept Catalina at his house while Ramon drove forty miles up the valley and made arrangements with a Mexican who lived in an isolated place, to care for her for an indefinite period. When he took Catalina there, he told her on the way simply that she was to wait until he came for her, and above all, that she must not try to communicate with her father. The girl nodded, looking at him gravely with her large soft eyes. Her lot had always been to obey, to bear burdens and to suffer. The stuff of rebellion and of self-assertion was not in her, but she could endure misfortune with the stoical indifference of a savage. Indeed, she was in all essentials simply a squaw. During the ride to her new home she seemed more interested in the novel sensation of travelling at thirty miles an hour than in her own future. She clung to the side of the car with both hands, and

[144]

her face reflected a pathetic mingling of fear and delight.

The house of Nestor Gomez to which Ramon took her was prettily set in a grove of cottonwoods, with white hollyhocks blooming on either side of the door, and strings of red chile hanging from the rafter-ends to dry. Half a dozen small children played about the door, the younger ones naked and all of them deep in dirt. A hen led her brood of chicks into the house on a foray for crumbs, and in the shade of the wall a mongrel bitch luxuriously gave teat to four pups. Bees humming about the hollyhocks bathed the scene in sleepy sound.

Catalina, utterly unembarassed, shook hands with her host and hostess in the limp, brief way of the Mexicans, and then, while Ramon talked with them, sat down in the shade, shook loose her heavy black hair and began to comb it. A little half-naked urchin of three years came and stood before her. She stopped combing to place her hands on his shoulders, and the two regarded each other long and intently, while Catalina's mouth framed a smile of dull wonder.

As Ramon drove back to town, he marvelled that he should ever have desired this clod of a woman; but he was grateful to her for the bovine calm with which she accepted things. He would visit her once in a while. He felt pretty sure that he could count on her not to make trouble.

Afterward he discussed the situation with Cortez. The latter was worried.

"You better look out," he counselled. "You better send him a message you are going to marry her. That will keep him quiet for a while. When he gets over being mad, maybe you can make him take a thousand dollars instead."

Ramon shook his head. If he gave Archulera to understand that he would marry the girl, word of it might get to town.

"He'll never find her," he said confidently. "I'll do nothing unless he comes to me."

"I don't know," Cortez replied doubtfully. "Is he a *penitente?*"

"Yes; I think he is," Ramon admitted.

"Then maybe he'll find her pretty quick. There are some *penitentes* still in the valley and all *penitentes* work together. You better look out."

CHAPTER XX

He had resolutely put the thought of Julia as much out of his mind as possible. He had conquered his disappointment at not being able to see her for a month, and had resolved to devote that month exclusively to hard work. And now came another one of those small, square, brief letters with its disturbing scent of lavender, and its stamp stuck upside down near the middle of the envelope.

"I will be in town tomorrow when you get this," she wrote, "But only for a day or two. We are going to move up to the capital for the rest of the year. Gordon is going to stay here now. Just mother and I are coming down to pack up our things. You can come and see me tomorrow evening."

It was astonishing, it was disturbing, it was incomprehensible. And it did not fit in with his plans. He had intended to go North and return before she did; then, with all his affairs in order, ask her to go away with him. Cortez had already sent word to Alfego that Ramon was coming to Arriba County. He could not afford a change of plans now. But the prospect of

[147]

seeing her again filled him with pleasure, sent a sort of weakening excitement tingling through his body.

And what did it mean that he was to be allowed to call on her? Had she, by any chance, won over her mother and brother? No; he couldn't believe it. But he went to her house that evening shaken by great hopes and anticipations.

She wore a black dress that left her shoulders bare, and set off the slim perfection of her little figure. Her face was flushed and her eyes were deep. How much more beautiful she was than the image he carried in his mind! He had been thinking of her all this while, and yet he had forgotten how beautiful she was. He could think of nothing to say at first, but held her by both hands and looked at her with eyes of wonder and desire. He felt a fool because his knees were weak and he was tremulous. But a happy fool! The touch and the sight of her seemed to dissolve his strength, and also the hardness and the bitterness that life had bred in him, the streak of animal ferocity that struggle brought out in him. He was all desire, but desire bathed in tenderness and hope. She made him feel as once long ago he had felt in church when the music and the pageantry and sweet odours of the place had filled his childish spirit with a strange sense of harmony. He had felt small and unworthy, yet happy and forgiven. So now he felt in her presence that he was black and bestial beside her, but that possession of her would somehow wash him clean and bring him peace.

When he tried to draw her to him she shook her head, not meeting his eyes and freed herself gently.

"No, no. I must tell you . . . " She led him to a seat, and went on, looking down at a toe that played with a design in the carpet. "I must explain. I promised mother that if she would let me see you this once to tell you, I would never try to see you again."

There was a long silence, during which he could feel his heart pounding and could see that she breathed quickly. Then suddenly he took her face in both hot hands and turned it toward him, made her meet his eyes.

"But of course you didn't mean that," he said.

She struggled weakly against his strength.

"I don't know. I thought I did. . . . It's terrible. You know. . . . I wrote you . . . some one saw us together. Gordon and mother found out about it. I won't tell you all that they said, but it was awful. It made me angry, and they found out that I love you. It had a terrible effect on Gordon. It made him worse. I can't tell you how awful it is for me. I love you. But I love him too. And to think I'm hurting him when he's sick, when I've lived in the hope he would get well. . . ."

She was breathing hard now. Her eyes were bright with tears. All her defences were down, her fine dignity vanished. When he took her in his arms she struggled a little at first; then yielded with closed eyes to his hot kisses.

Afterward they talked a little, but not to much purpose. He had important things to tell her, they had plans to make. But their great disturbing hunger for each other would not let them think of anything else. Their conversation was always interrupted by hot confusing embraces.

The clock struck eleven, and she jumped up.

"I promised to make you go home at eleven," she told him.

"But I must tell you . . . I have to leave town for a while." He found his tongue suddenly. Briefly he outlined the situation he faced with regard to his estate. Of course, he said nothing about the *penitentes*, but he made her understand that he was going forth to fight for both their fortunes.

"I can't do it, I won't go, unless I know I am to have you," he finished. "Everything I have done, everything I am going to do is for you. If I lose you I lose everything. You promise to go with me?"

His eyes were burning with earnestness, and

hers were wide with admiration. He did not really understand her, nor she him. Unalterable differences of race and tradition and temperament stood between them. They had little in common save a great primitive hunger. But that, none-the-less, for the moment genuinely transfigured and united them.

She drew a deep breath.

"Yes. You must promise not to try to see me until then. When you are ready, let me know."

She threw back her head, opening her arms to him. For a moment she hung limp in his embrace; then pushed him away and ran upstairs, leaving him to find his way out alone.

He walked home slowly, trying to straighten out his thoughts. Her presence seemed still to be all about him. One of her hairs was tangled about a button of his coat; her powder and the scent of her were all over his shoulder; the recollection of her kisses smarted sweetly on his mouth. He was weak, confused, ridiculously happy. But he knew that he would carry North with him greater courage and purpose than ever before he had known.

CHAPTER XXI

In the dry clean air of the Southwest all things change slowly. Growth is slow and decay is even slower. The body of a dead horse in the desert does not rot but dessicates, the hide remaining intact for months, the bones perhaps for years. Men and beasts often live to great age. The *pinon* trees on the red hills were there when the conquerors came, and they are not much larger now—only more gnarled and twisted.

This strange inertia seems to possess institutions and customs as well as life itself. In the valley towns, it is true, the railroads have brought and thrown down all the conveniences and incongruities of civilization. But ride away from the railroads into the mountains or among the lava *mesas,* and you are riding into the past. You will see little earthen towns, brown or golden or red in the sunlight, according to the soil that bore them, which have not changed in a century. You will see grain threshed by herds of goats and ponies driven around and around the threshing floors, as men threshed grain before the Bible was written. You will see Indian pueblos which have not changed materially since the brave days when

Coronado came to Taos and the Spanish soldiers
stormed the heights of Acoma. You will hear
of strange Gods and devils and of the evil eye.
It is almost as though this crystalline air were
indeed a great clear crystal, impervious to time,
in which the past is forever encysted.

The region in which Ramon's heritage lay was
a typical part of this forgotten land. In the
southern end of the Rocky Mountains, it was a
country of great tilted *mesas* reaching above
timber line, covered for the most part with heavy
forests of pine and fir, with here and there great
upland pastures swept clean by forest fires of
long ago. Along the lower slopes of the mountains, where the valleys widened, were primitive
little *adobe* towns, in which the Mexicans lived,
each owning a few acres of tillable land. In the
summer they followed their sheep herds in the
upland pastures. There were not a hundred
white men in the whole of Arriba County, and no
railroad touched it.

In this region a few Mexicans who were
shrewder or stronger than the others, who owned
stores or land, dominated the rest of the people
much as the *patrones* had dominated them in the
days before the Mexican War. Here still
flourished the hatred for the gringo which cul-
minated in that war. Here that strange sect, the
penitentes hermanos, half savage and half me-

diaeval, still was strong and still recruited its strength every year with young men, who elsewhere were refusing to undergo its brutal tortures.

For all of these reasons, this was an advantageous field for the fight Ramon proposed to make. In the valley MacDougall's money and influence would surely have beaten him. But here he could play upon the ancient hatred for the gringo; here he could use to the best advantage the prestige of his family; here, above all, if he could win over the *penitentes,* he could do almost any thing he pleased.

His plan of joining that ancient order to gain influence was not an original one. Mexican politicians and perhaps one or two gringos had done it, and the fact was a matter of common gossip. Some of these *penitentes* for a purpose had been men of great influence, and their initiations had been tempered to suit their sensitive skins. Others had been Mexicans of the poorer sort, capable of sharing the half-fanatic, half sadistic spirit of the thing.

Ramon came to the order as a young and almost unknown man seeking its aid. He could not hope for much mercy. And though he was primitive in many ways, there was nothing in him that responded to the spirit of this ordeal. The thought of Christ crucified did not inspire him to endure suffering. But the thought of a girl with yellow hair did.

CHAPTER XXII

Ramon went first to the ranch at the foot of the mountains which his uncle had used as a head-quarters, and which had belonged to the family for about half a century. It consisted merely of an *adobe* ranch house and barn and a log corral for rounding up horses.

Here Ramon left his machine. Here also he exchanged his business suit for corduroys, a wide hat and high-heeled riding boots. He greatly fancied himself in this costume and he embellished it with a silk bandana of bright scarlet and with a large pair of silver spurs which had belonged to his uncle, and which he found in the saddle room of the barn. From the accoutrement in this room he also selected the most pretentious-looking saddle. It was a heavy stock saddle, with German silver mountings and saddle bags covered with black bear fur. A small red and black Navajo blanket served as a saddle pad and he found a fine Navajo bridle, too, woven of black horsehair, with a big hand-hammered silver buckle on each cheek.

He had the old Mexican who acted as caretaker for the ranch drive all of the ranch horses into the corral, and chose a spirited roan mare for a saddle animal. He always rode a roan horse when he could get one because a roan mustang has more spirit than one of any other colour.

The most modern part of his equipment was his weapon. He did not want to carry one openly, so he had purchased a small but highly efficient automatic pistol, which he wore in a shoulder scabbard inside his shirt and under his left elbow.

When his preparations were completed he rode straight to the town of Alfego where the powerful Solomon had his establishment, dismounted under the big cottonwoods and strolled into the long, dark cluttered *adobe* room which was Solomon Alfego's store. Three or four Mexican clerks were waiting upon as many Mexican customers, with much polite, low-voiced conversation, punctuated by long silences while the customers turned the goods over and over in their hands. Ramon's entrance created a slight diversion. None of them knew him, for he had not been in that country for years, but all of them recognized that he was a person of weight and importance. He saluted all at once, lifting his hat, with a cordial *"Como lo va, amigos,"* and then devoted himself to an apparently interested inspection of the stock. This, if conscientiously done, would have afforded a week's occupation, for Solomon Alfego served as sole merchant for a large territory and had to be prepared to supply almost every human want. There were shelves of dry goods and of hardware, of tobacco and of medicines. In the centre of the store was a long rack, heavily laden with saddlery and harness of all kinds, and all around the top of the room, above the shelves, ran a row of religious pictures, including popes, saints, and cardinals, Mary with the infant, Christ crucified and Christ bearing the cross, all done in bright colours and framed, for sale at about three dollars each.

It was not long before word of the stranger's arrival reached Alfego in his little office behind the store, and he came bustling out, beaming and polite.

"This is Senor Solomon Alfego?" Ramon enquired in his most formal Spanish.

"I am Solomon Alfego," replied the bulky little man, with a low bow, "and what can I do for the Senor?"

"I am Ramon Delcasar," Ramon replied, extending his hand with a smile, "and it may be that you can do much for me."

"Ah-h-h!" breathed Alfego, with another bow, "Ramon Delcasar! And I knew you when you were *un muchachito*" (a little boy). He bent over and measured scant two feet from the floor with his hand. "My house is yours. I am at your service. *Siempre!*"

The two strolled about the store, talking of the weather, politics, business, the old days— everything except what they were both thinking about. Alfego opened a box of cigars, and having lit a couple of these, they went out on the long porch and sat down on an old buggy seat to continue the conversation. Alfego admired Ramon's horse and especially his silver-mounted saddle.

"Ha! you like the saddle!" Ramon exclaimed in well-stimulated delight. He rose, swiftly undid the cinches, and dropped saddle and blanket at the feet of his host. "It is yours!" he announced.

"A thousand thanks," Alfego replied. "Come; I wish to show you some Navajo blankets I bought the other day." He led the way into the store, and directed one of his clerks to bring forth a great stack of the heavy Indian weaves, and began turning them over. They were blankets of the best quality, and some of the designs in red, black and grey were of exceptional beauty. Ramon stood smiling while his host turned over one blanket after another. As he displayed each one he turned his bright pop-eyes on Ramon with an eager enquiring look. At last when he had

[158]

seen them all, Ramon permitted himself to pick up and examine the one he considered the best with a restrained murmur of admiration.

"You like it!" exclaimed Alfego with delight. "It is yours!"

Mutual good feeling having thus been signalized in the traditional Mexican manner by an exchange of gifts, Alfego now showed his guest all over his establishment. It included, in addition to the store, several ware rooms where were piled stinking bales of sheep and goat and cow hides, sacks of raw wool and of corn, pelts of wild animals and bags of *pinon* nuts, and of beans, all taken from the Mexicans in trade. Afterward Ramon met the family, of patriarchal proportions, including an astonishing number of little brown children having the bright eyes and well developed noses of the great Solomon. Then came supper, a long and bountiful feast, at which great quantities of mutton, chile, and beans were served.

Having thus been duly impressed with the greatness and substance of his host, and also with his friendly attitude, Ramon was led into the little office, offered a seat and a fresh cigar. He knew that at last the proper time had come for him to declare himself.

"My friend," he said, leaning toward Alfego confidentially, "I have come to this country and to you for a great purpose. You know that a rich gringo has been buying the lands of the poor people—my people and yours—all through this country. You know that he intends to own all of this country—to take it away from us Mexicans. If he succeeds, he will take away all of your business, all of my lands. You and I must fight him together. Am I right?"

Solomon nodded his head slowly, watching Ramon with wide bright eyes.

"*Verdad!*" he pronounced unctuously.

"I have come," Ramon went on more boldly, "because my own lands are in danger, but also because I love the Mexican people, and hate the gringos! Some one must go among these good people and warn them not to sell their lands, not to be cheated out of their birthrights. My friend, I have come here to do that."

"*Bueno!*" exclaimed Alfego. "*Muy bueno!*"

"My friend, I must have your help."

Ramon said this as impressively as possible, and paused expectantly, but as Alfego said nothing, he went on, gathering his wits for the supreme effort.

"I know that you are a leader in the great fraternity of the penitent brothers, who are the best and most pious of men. My friend, I wish to become one of them. I wish to mingle my blood with theirs and with the blood of Christ, that all of us may be united in our great purpose

[160]

to keep this country for the Spanish people, who conquered it from the barbarians."

Alfego looked very grave, puffed his cigar violently three times and spat before he answered.

"My young friend," (he spoke slowly and solemnly) "to pour out your blood in penance and to consecrate your body to Christ is a great thing to do. Have you meditated deeply upon this step? Are you sure the Lord Jesus has called you to his service? And what assurance have I that you are sincere in all you say, that if I make you my brother in the blood of Christ, you will truly be as a brother to me?"

Ramon bowed his head.

"I have thought long on this," he said softly, "and I know my heart. I desire to be a blood brother to all these, my people. And to you— I give you my word as a Delcasar that I will serve you well, that I will be as a brother to you."

There was a silence during which Alfego stared with profound gravity at the ash on the end of his cigar.

"Have you heard," Ramon went on, in the same soft and emotional tone of voice, "that the Denver and Rio Grande Railroad is going to build a line through the San Antonio Valley?"

Alfego, without altering his look of rapt meditation, nodded his head slowly.

[161]

"Do you suppose that you will gain anything by that, if this gringo gets these lands?" Ramon went on. "You know that you will not. But I will make you my partner. And I will give you the option on any of my mountain land that you may wish to rent for sheep range. More than that, I will make you a written agreement to do these things. In all ways we will be as brothers."

"You are a worthy and pious young man!" exclaimed Solomon Alfego, rolling his eyes upward, his voice vibrant with emotion. "You shall be my brother in the blood of Christ."

CHAPTER XXIII

Ramon went to the *Morada,* the chapter house of the *penitentes,* alone and late at night, for all of the whippings and initiations of the order, except those of Holy Week, are carried on in the utmost secrecy.

The *Morada* stood halfway up the slope north of the little town, at the elevation where the tall yellow pines of the mountains begin to replace the scrubby juniper and *pinon* of the *mesas* and foothills. It was a cool moonlit night of late summer. A light west wind breathed through the trees, making the massive black shadows of the juniper bushes faintly alive. As he toiled up the rocky path Ramon heard the faraway yap and yodel of a coyote, and the still more distant answer of another one. From the valley below came the intermittent bay of a cur, inspired by the moon and his wild kin, and now and then the tiny silver tinkle of a goat bell.

The *Morada* stood in an open space. It was an oblong block of *adobe,* and gave forth neither light nor sound. Ramon stopped a little way from it in the shadow of a tree and lit a cigarette to steady his nerves. He felt now for the first

[163]

time something of the mystery and terribleness of this barbaric order which he proposed to use for his purpose. All his life the *penitentes* had been to him a well-known fact of life. For the past week he had spent much of his time with the *maestro de novios* of the local chapter, a wizened old sheep herder, who had instructed him monotonously in the secrets of the order, almost lulling him to sleep with his endless mumblings of the ritual that was written in a little leather book a century old. He had learned that if he betrayed the secrets of the order, he would be buried alive with only his head sticking out of the ground, so that the ants might eat his face. He had been informed that if he fell ill he would be taken to the *Morada* where his brothers in Christ would pray for him, and seek to drive the devil out of his body, and that if he died, they would send his shoes to his family as a notice of that event; and would bury him in consecrated ground. Some of the things he had learned had bored him and some had made him want to laugh, but none of them had impressed him, as they were intended to do, with the might and dignity of the ancient order.

He was impressed now as he stood before this dark still house where a dozen ignorant fanatics waited to take his blood for what was to them a holy purpose. He knew that this *Morada* was a very old one. He thought of all the true penitents who had knocked for admission at its door and had gone through its bloody ordeal with a zeal of madness which had enabled them to cry loudly for blows and more blows until they fell insensible. He tried to imagine their state of mind, but he could not. He was of their race and a growth of the same soil, but an alien civilization had touched him and sundered him from them, yet without taking him for its own. He could only nerve himself to face this ordeal because it would serve his one great purpose.

As he stood there, a curious half-irrelevant thought came into his mind. He knew that the marks they would make on his back would be permanent. He had seen the long rough scars on the backs of sheep-herders, stripped to the waist for the hot work of shearing. And he wondered how he would explain these strange scars to Julia. He imagined her discovering them with her long dainty hands, her round white arms. A great longing surged up in him that seemed to weaken the very tissues of his body. He shook himself, threw away his cigarette, went to the heavy wooden door and knocked.

Now he spoke a rigamarole in Spanish which had been taught him by rote.

"God knocks at this mission's door for His clemency," he called.

From within came a deep-voiced chorus, the first sound he had heard from the house, seeming weirdly to be the voice of the house itself.

"Penance, penance, which seeks salvation!" it chanted.

"Saint Peter will open to me the gate, bathing me with the light, in the name of Mary, with the seal of Jesus," Ramon went on, repeating as he had learned. "I ask this confraternity. Who gives this house light?"

"Jesus," answered the chorus within.

"Who fills it with joy?"

"Mary."

"Who preserves it with faith?"

"Joseph!"

The door opened and Ramon entered the chapel room of the *Morada*. It was lighted by a single candle, which revealed dimly the rough earthen walls, the low roof raftered with round pine logs, the wooden benches and the altar, covered with black cloth. This was decorated with figures of the skull and cross-bones cut from white cloth. A human skull stood on either side of it, and a small wooden crucifix hung on the wall above it. The solitary candle—an ordinary tallow one in a tin holder—stood before this.

The men were merely dark human shapes. The light did not reveal their faces. They said nothing to Ramon. He could scarcely believe

[166]

that these were the same good-natured *pelados* he had known by day. Indeed they were not the same, but were now merely units of this organization which held them in bondage of fear and awe.

One of them took Ramon silently by the arm and led him through a low door into the other room which was the *Morada* proper. This room was supposed never to be entered except by a member of the order or by a candidate. It was small and low as the other, furnished only with a few benches about the wall, and lighted by a couple of candles on a small table. A very old and tarnished oil painting of Mary with the Babe hung at one end of it. All the way around the room, hanging from pegs driven into the wall, was a row of the broad heavy braided lashes of *amole* weed, called *disciplinas*, used in Holy Week, and of the blood-stained drawers worn on that occasion by the flagellants.

Still in complete silence Ramon was forced to his knees by two of the men, who quickly stripped him to the waist. Beside him stood a tall powerfully-built Mexican with his right arm bared. In his hand he held a triangular bit of white quartz, cleverly chipped to a cutting edge. This man was the *sangredor,* whose duty it was to place the seal of the order upon the penitent's back. His office required no little skill, for he had to make three cuts the whole length of the back and three

the width, tearing through the skin so as to leave
a permanent scar, but not deep enough to injure
the muscle. Ramon, glancing up, saw the gleam
of the candle light on the white quartz, and also
in the eyes of the man, which were bright with
eagerness.

Now came the supreme struggle with himself.
How could he go through with this ugly agony?
He longed to leap to his feet and fight these
ignorant louts, who were going to mangle him
and beat him for their own amusement. He
held himself down with all his will, striving to
think of the girl, to hold his purpose before his
mind, to endure...

He felt the hand of the *sangredor* upon his
neck, and gritted his teeth. The man's grip was
heavy, hot and firm. A flash of pain shot up and
down his back with lightning speed, as though a
red hot poker had been laid upon it. Again and
again and again! Six times in twice as many
seconds the deft flint ripped his skin, and he fell
forward upon his hands, faint and sick, as he
felt his own blood welling upon his back and
trickling in warm rivulets between his ribs.

But this was not all. To qualify, he knew, he
must call for the lash of his own free will.

"For the love of God," he uttered painfully,
as he had been taught, "the three meditations of
the passion of our Lord."

[168]

On his torn back a long black snake whip came down, wielded with merciless force. But he felt the full agony of the first blow only. The second seemed faint, and the third sent him plunging downward through a red mist into black nothingness.

CHAPTER XXIV

A few days later one bright morning Ramon was sitting in the sun before the door of his friend, Francisco Guiterrez, feeling still somewhat sore, but otherwise surprisingly well. Guiterrez, a young sheep-herder, held the position of *coadjutor* of the local *penitente* chapter, and one of his duties as such was to take the penitent to his house and care for him after the initiation. He had washed Ramon's wounds in a tea made by boiling Romero weed. This was a remedy which the *penitentes* had used for centuries, and its efficacy was proved by the fact that Ramon's cuts had begun to heal at once, and that he had had very little fever.

For a couple of days Ramon had been forced to lie restlessly in the only bed of the Guiterrez establishment. The Senora Guiterrez, a pretty buxom young Mexican woman, had fed him on *atole* gruel and on all of the eggs which her small flock of scrub hens produced; the seven little dirty brown Guiterrez children had come in to marvel at him with their fingers in their mouths; the Guiterrez goats and dogs and chickens had wandered in and out of the room in a companionable way, as though seeking to make him feel at ease; and Guiterrez himself had spent his evenings sitting beside Ramon, smoking cigarettes and talking.

This time of idleness had not been wholly wasted, either, for it had come out in the course of conversation that Guiterrez had been offered a thousand dollars for his place by a man whom he did not know, but whom Ramon had easily identified as an agent of MacDougall. Tempted by an amount which he could scarcely conceive, Guiterrez was thinking seriously of accepting the offer.

Now that he had won over Alfego and had gotten the influence of the *penitentes* on his side, Ramon's one remaining object was to defeat just such deals as this, which MacDougall already had under way. He intended to stir up feeling against the gringos, and to persuade the Mexicans not to sell. Later, such lands as he needed in order to control the right-of-way, he would gain by lending money and taking mortgages. But he did not intend to cheat any one. Such Mexicans as he had to oust from their lands, he would locate elsewhere. He was filled with a large generosity, and with a real love for these, his people. He meant to dominate this country,

[171]

but his pride demanded that no one should be poor or hungry in his domain. So now he argued the matter to Guiterrez with real sincerity.

"A thousand dollars? *Por Dios,* man! Don't you know that this place is worth many thousand dollars to you?"

"How can it be worth many thousand?" Guiterrez demanded. "What have I here? A few acres of chile and corn, a little hay, some range for my goats, a few cherry trees, a house. . . . Many thousands? No."

"You have here a home, *amigo,*" Ramon reminded him. "Do you know how long a thousand dollars would support you? A year, perhaps. Then you would have to work for other men the rest of your life. Here you are free and independent."

Guiterrez said nothing, but he had obviously received a new idea, and was impressed. Ramon never returned to the direct argument, but he missed no chance to stimulate Guiterrez's pride in his establishment.

"This is a good little house you have *amigo,*" he would observe. And Guiterrez would tell him that the house had been built by his grandfather, but that its walls were as firm as ever, and that he had been intending for several years to plaster it, but had never gotten time. Before he was out of bed, Ramon was reasonably sure that Guiterrez would never sell.

The house was indeed charmingly situated on a hillside at the foot of which a little clear trout stream, called Rio Gallinas, chuckled over the bright pebbles in its bed and ran to hide in thickets of willow.

Sitting on the *portal,* which ran the length of the house and consisted of a projection of the roof supported by rough pine logs, Ramon could look down the canyon to where it widened into a little valley that lost itself in the vast levels of the *mesa.* There thirsty sands swallowed the stream and not a sprig of green marred the harmony of grey and purple swimming in vivid light, reaching away to the horizon where faint blue mountains hung in drooping lines.

By turning his head, Ramon could look into the heart of the mountains whence the stream issued through a narrow canyon, with steep, forested ridges on either side, and little level glades along the water, set with tall, conical blue spruce trees, pines with their warm red boles, and little clumps of aspen with gleaming white stems, and trembling leaves of mingled gold and green.

Ramon spent many hours with his back against the wall, his knees drawn up under his chin, Mexican fashion, smoking and vaguely dreaming of

[173]

the girl he loved and of the things he would do.
The vast sun drenched landscape before him was
too much a part of his life, too intimate a thing
for him to appreciate its beauty, but after his
struggles with doubt and desire, it filled him with
an unaccountable contentment. Its warmth and
brightness, its unchanging serenity, its ceaseless
soft voices of wind and water, lulled his mind and
comforted his senses. The country was like some
great purring creature that let him lie in its
bosom and filled his body with the warm steady
throb of its untroubled strength.

After a week of recuperation, he bought a
horse from Guiterrez for a pack animal, loaded
it with bedding and provisions and rode away
into the mountains. His task was now to find
other men who had fallen under the influence of
MacDougall, and to persuade them not to sell
their lands. Some of them would be at their
homes, but others would be with the sheep herds,
scattered here and there in the high country.
He faced long days of mountain wandering, and
for all that he longed to be done with his task,
this part of it was sweet to him.

CHAPTER XXV

These were days of power and success, days of a glamour that lingered long in his mind. Beyond a doubt he was destroying MacDougall's plan and realizing his own. Sometimes he met a surly Mexican who would not listen to him, but nearly always he won the man over in the end. He was amazed at his own resourcefulness and eloquence. It seemed as though some inhibition in him had been broken down, some magical elixir poured into his imagination. He found that he could literally take a sheep camp by storm, entering into the life of the men, telling them stories, singing them songs, passing out presents of tobacco and whisky, often delivering a wildly applauded harangue on the necessity for all Mexicans to act together against the gringos, who would otherwise soon own the country. Never once did he think of the incongruity of thus fanning the flames of race hatred for the love of a girl with grey eyes and yellow hair.

He did not always reach a house or a sheep camp at night. Many a time he camped alone, catching trout for his supper from a mountain stream, and going to sleep to the lonely music of running water in a wilderness. At such times many a man would have lost faith in himself, would have feared his crimes and lost his hopes. But to Ramon this loneliness was an old friend. Like all who have lived much out-of-doors he was at heart a pantheist, and felt more at peace and unity with wild nature than ever he had with men.

But there was one such night when he felt troubled. As he rode up the Tusas Canyon at twilight, a sense of insecurity came over him, amounting almost to fear. He had had a somewhat similar feeling once when a panther had trailed him on a winter night. Now, as then, he had no idea what it was that menaced him; he was simply warned by that sixth sense which belongs to all wild things, and to men in whom there remains something of the feral. His horses shared his unrest. When he picketed them, just before dark, they fed uneasily, stopping now and then to stand like statues with lifted heads, testing the wind with their nostrils, moving their ears to catch some sound beyond human perception.

When he had eaten his supper and made his bed, Ramon took the little automatic revolver out of its scabbard and went down the canyon a quarter of a mile, slipping along in the shadow of the brush that lined the banks of the stream. This was necessary because a half-moon made the open glades bright. He paused and peered a dozen times. So cautious were his movements that he came within forty feet of a drinking deer, and was badly startled when it bounded away with a snort and a smashing of brush. But he saw nothing dangerous and went back to his camp and to bed. There he lay awake for an hour, still troubled, oppressed by a vague feeling of the littleness and insecurity of human life.

A long, rippling snort of fear from his saddle horse, picketed near his bed, awakened him and probably saved his life. When he opened his eyes, he saw the figure of a man standing directly over him. He was about to speak, when the man lifted his arms, swinging upward a heavy club. With quick presence of mind, Ramon jerked the blankets and the heavy canvas tarpaulin about his head, at the same time rolling over. The club came down with crushing force on his right shoulder. He continued to roll and flounder with all his might, going down a sharp slope toward the creek which was only a few yards away. Twice more he felt the club, once on his arm and once on his ribs, but his head escaped and the heavy blankets protected his body.

The next thing he knew, he had gone over the bank of the creek, which was several feet high in that place, and lay in the shallow icy water. Meantime he had gotten his hand on the automatic pistol. He now jerked upright and fired at the form of his assailant, which bulked above him. The man disappeared. For a moment Ramon sat still. He heard footsteps, and something like a grunt or a groan. Then he extricated himself from the cold, sodden blankets, climbed upon the bank, and began cautiously searching about, with his weapon ready. He found the club—a heavy length of green spruce—and put his hand accidentally on something wet, which he ascertained by smelling it to be blood.

He was shivering with cold and badly bruised in several places, but he was afraid to build a fire. In case his enemy were not badly injured or had a companion, that would have been risking another attack. He stood in the shadow of a spruce, stamping his feet and rubbing himself, acutely uncomfortable, waiting for daylight and wondering what this attack meant. He doubted whether MacDougall would have countenanced such tactics, but it might well have been an agent of MacDougall acting on his own responsibility. Or it might have been some one sent by old Archulera. Then, too, there were many poor connections of the Delcasar family who would profit by his death.

As he stood there in the dark, shivering and miserable, the idea of death was not hard for him to conceive. He realized that but for the snort of the saddle horse he would now be lying under the tree with the top of his head crushed in. The man would probably have dragged his body into the thick timber and left it.   There he would have lain and rotted.   Or perhaps the coyotes would have eaten him and the buzzards afterward picked his bones.   He shuddered.   Despite his acute misery, life had never seemed more desirable. He thought of sunlight and warmth, of good food and of the love of women, and these things seemed more sweet than ever before.   He realized, for the first time, too, that he faced many dangers and that the chance of death walked with him all the time.   He resolved fiercely that he would beat all his enemies, that he would live and have his desires which were so sweet to him.

Daylight came at last, showing him first the rim of the mountain serrated with spruce tops, and then lighting the canyon, revealing his disordered camp and his horses grazing quietly in the open.   He went immediately and examined the ground where the struggle had taken place. A plain trail of blood lead away from the place, as he had expected.   He formed a plan of action immediately.

First he made a great fire, dried and warmed himself, cooked and ate his breakfast, drinking a full pint of hot coffee.   Then he rolled up all his belongings, hid them in the bushes, and picketed his horses in a side canyon where the grass was good.   When these preparations were complete,

[179]

he took the trail of blood and followed it with the utmost care. He carried his weapon cocked in his hand, and always before he went around a bend in the canyon, or passed through a clump of trees, he paused and looked long and carefully, like an animal stalking dangerous prey.

At last, from the cover of some willows, he saw a man sitting beside the creek. The man was half-naked, and was binding up his leg with some strips torn from his dirty shirt. He was a Mexican of the lowest and most brutal type, with a swarthy skin, black hair and a bullet-shaped head. Ramon walked toward him.

"*Buenas Dias, amigo*," he saluted.

The man looked up with eyes full of patient suffering, like the eyes of a hurt animal. He did not seem either surprised or frightened. He nodded and went on binding up his leg.

Ramon watched him a minute. He saw that the man was weak from loss of blood. There was a great patch of dried blood on the ground beside him, now beginning to flake and curl in the sun.

"I will come back in a minute, friend," he said.

He went back to his camp, saddled his horses, putting some food in the saddle pockets. When he returned, the Mexican sat in exactly the same place with his back against a rock and his legs and arms inert. Ramon fried bacon and made coffee for him. He had to help the man put the food in his mouth and hold a cup for him to drink. Afterward, with great difficulty, he loaded the man on his saddle horse, where he sat heavily, clutching the pommel with both hands. Ramon mounted the pack horse bareback.

"Where do you live, friend?" Ramon asked.

"Tusas," the Mexican replied, naming a little village ten miles down the canyon.

They exchanged no other words until they came within sight of the group of *adobe* houses. Then Ramon stopped his horse and turned to the man.

"You were hunting," he told him slowly and impressively, "and you dropped your gun and shot yourself. *Sabes?*"

The man nodded.

"How much were you paid to kill me, friend?" Ramon then asked.

The man looked at the pommel of the saddle, and his swarthy face darkened with a heavy flush.

"One hundred dollars," he admitted. "I needed the money to christen a child. Could I let my child go to hell? But I did not mean to kill you. Only to beat you, so you would go away. Do not ask who sent me, for the love of God. . . ."

"I ask nothing more, friend," Ramon assured

[181]

him. "And since you were to have a hundred dollars for making me leave the country, here is a hundred dollars for not succeeding."

Both of them laughed. Ramon then rode on and delivered the man to his excited and grateful wife. He went back to his camp very weary and sore, but feeling that he had done an excellent stroke of work for his purpose.

CHAPTER XXVI

After this occurrence his success among the humbler Mexicans was more marked than ever, but some of the men of property who had been subsidized by MacDougall were not so easily won over. Such a case was that of old Pedro Alcatraz who owned a little store in the town of Vallecitos, a bit of land and a few thousand sheep. Alcatraz was a tall boney old man, and was of nearly pure Navajo Indian blood, as one could tell by the queer crinkled character of his beard and moustache, which were like those of a chinaman. He was simple and direct like an Indian, too, lacking the Mexican talent for lying and artifice. In his own town he was a petty czar, like Alfego, but on a much smaller scale. By reason of being *Hermano Mayor* of the local *penitente* chapter, and of having most of the people in his own neighbourhood in debt to him, he had considerable power. He was advising men to sell their lands, and was lending more money on land than it was reasonable to suppose he owned. Beyond a doubt, he had been won by MacDougall's dollars.

Ramon found Alcatraz unresponsive. The old man listened to a long harangue on the subject of the race issue without a word of reply, and without looking up. Ramon then played what should have been his strongest card.

"My friend," he said, "you may not know it, but I am your brother in the blood of Christ. Do I not then deserve better of you than a gringo who is trying to take this country away from the Mexican people?"

"Yes," the old man answered quietly, "I know you are a *penitente,* and I know why. Do you think that I am a fool like these *pelados* that herd my sheep? You wear the scars of a *penitente* because you think it will help you to make money and to do what you want. You are just like MacDougall, except that he uses money and you use words. A poor man can only choose his masters, and for my part I have more use for money than for words." So saying, the blunt old savage walked to the other end of his store and began showing a Mexican woman some shawls.

Ramon went away, breathing hard with rage, slapping his quirt against his boots. He would show that old *cabron* who was boss in these mountains!

He went immediately and hired the little *adobe* hall which is found in every Mexican town of more than a hundred inhabitants, and made preparations to give a *baile.*

To give a dance is the surest and simplest way

to win popularity in a Mexican town, and Ramon spared no expense to make this affair a success. He sent forty miles across the mountains for two fiddlers to help out the blind man who was the only local musician. He arranged a feast, and in a back room he installed a small keg of native wine and one of beer.

The invitation was general and every one who could possibly reach the place in a day's journey came. The women wore for the most part calico dresses, bright in colour and generous in volume, heavily starched and absolutely devoid of fit. Their brown faces were heavily powdered, producing in some of the darker ones a purplish tint, which was ghastly in the light of the oil lamps. Some of the younger girls were comely despite their crude toilets, with soft skins, ripe breasts, mild dark heifer-like eyes, and pretty teeth showing in delighted grins. The men wore the cheap ready-made suits which have done so much to make Americans look alike everywhere, but they achieved a degree of originality by choosing brighter colours than men generally wear, being especially fond of brilliant electric blues and rich browns. Their broad but often handsome faces were radiant with smiles, and their thick black hair was wetted and greased into shiny order.

The dance started with difficulty, despite symptoms of eagerness on all hands. Bashful youths

[185]

stalled and crowded in the doorway like a log jam in the river. Bashful girls, seated all around the room, nudged and tittered and then became solemn and self-conscious. Each number was preceded by a march, several times around the room, which was sedate and formal in the extreme. The favourite dance was a fast, hopping waltz, in which the swain seized his partner firmly in both hands under the arms and put her through a vigorous test of wind and agility. The floor was rough and sanded, and the rasping of feet almost drowned the music. There were long Virginia reels, led with peremptory dash by a master of ceremonies, full of grace and importance. Swarthy faces were bedewed with sweat and dark eyes glowed with excitement, but there was never the slightest relaxation of the formalism of the affair. For this dance in an earthen hovel on a plank floor was the degenerate but lineal descendant of the splendid and formal balls which the Dons had held in the old days, when New Spain belonged to its proud and wealthy conquerors; it was the wistful and grotesque remnant of a dying order.

Ramon had a vague realization of this fact as he watched the affair. It stirred a sort of sentimental pity in him. But he threw off that feeling, he had work to do. He entered into the spirit of the thing, dancing with every woman on the floor. He took the men in groups to the back room and treated them. He missed no opportunity to get in a word against the gringos, and incidentally against those Mexicans who betrayed their fellows by advising them to sell their lands. He never mentioned Alcatraz by name, but he made it clear enough to whom he referred.

Late in the evening, when all were mellowed by drink and excited by dancing, he gained the attention of the gathering on the pretext of announcing a special dance, and boldly gave a harangue in which he urged all Mexicans to stick together against the gringos, and above all not to sell their homes which their fathers had won from the barbarians, and were the foundations of their prosperity and freedom.

"Remember," he urged them in a burst of eloquence that surprised himself, "that in your veins is the blood of conquerors—blood which was poured out on these hills and valleys to win them from the Indians, precious blood which has made this land priceless to you for all time!"

His speech was greeted with a burst of applause unquestionably spontaneous. It filled him with a sense of power that was almost intoxicating. In the town he might be neglected, despised, picked for an easy mark, but here among his own people he was a ruler and leader by birth.

The most important result of the *baile* was that

CHAPTER XXVII

A week later Ramon was driving across the *mesa* west of town, bound for the state capital. He was following the same route that Diego Delcasar had followed on the day of his death, and he passed within a few miles of Archulera's ranch; but no thought either of his uncle or of Archulera entered his mind. For in his pocket was a letter consisting of a single sentence hastily scrawled in a large round upright hand on lavender-scented note paper. The sentence was:

"Meet you at the southwest corner of the Plaza Tuesday at seven thirty.

"Love,
"J. R."

A great deal of trouble and anxiety had preceded the receipt of that message. First he had written her a letter that was unusually long and exuberant for him, telling her of his success and that now he was ready to come and get her in accordance with their agreement, suggesting a time and place. Three days of cumulative doubt and agony had gone by without a reply. Then he had tried to reach her by long distance telephone, but without success. Finally he had wired, although he knew that a telegram is a risky vehicle for confidential business. Now he had her answer, the answer that he wanted. His spirit was released and leapt forward, leaving resentments and doubts far behind.

It was eighty miles to the state capital, the road was good all the way, the day bright and cool. His route lead across the *mesa,* through the Scissors Pass, and then north and east along the foot of the mountains.

Immense and empty the country stretched before him,—a land of far-flung levels and even farther mountains; a land which makes even the sea, with its near horizons, seem little; a land which has always produced men of daring because it inspires a sense of freedom without any limit save what daring sets.

He had dared and won. He was going to take the sweet price of his daring. The engine of his big car sang to him a song of victory and desire. He rejoiced in the sense of power under his hand. He opened the throttle wider and the car answered with more speed, licking up the road like a hungry monster. How easily he mastered time and distance for his purpose!

He was to have her, she would be his. So sang the humming motor and the wind in his ears. Her white arms and her red mouth, her splendid

[190]

eyes that feared and yielded! She was waiting for him! More speed. He conquered the hills with a roar of strength to spare, topped the crests, and sped down the long slopes like a bird coming to earth.

He was to have her, she would be his. Could it be true? The great machine that carried him to their tryst roared an affirmative, the wind sang of it, his blood quickened with anticipation incredibly keen. And always the distance that lay between them was falling behind in long, grey passive miles.

He had reached his destination a little after six. As he drove slowly through the streets of the little dusty town, the mood of exaltation that had possessed him during the trip died down. He was intent, worried practical. Having registered at the hotel, he got a handful of time tables and made his plans with care. They would drive to a town twenty-five miles away, be married, and catch the California Limited. There would just be time. Once he had her in his car, nothing could stop them.

The *plaza* or public square about which the old town was built, and which had been its market place in the old days, was now occupied by a neat little park with a band stand. Retail stores and banks fronted on three sides of it, but the fourth was occupied by a long low *adobe* building

which was very old and had been converted into a
museum of local antiquities. It was dark and
lifeless at night, and in its shadow-filled verandah
he was to meet her.

He had his car parked beside the spot ten minutes ahead of time. It was slightly cold now,
with a gusty wind whispering about the streets
and tearing big papery leaves from the cottonwood trees in the park. The *plaza* was empty
save for an occasional passer-by whose quick foot-
falls rang sharply in the silence. Here and there
was an illuminated shop window. The drug
store on the opposite corner showed a bright in-
terior, where two small boys devoured ice cream
sodas with solemn rapture. Somewhere up a
side street a choir was practising a hymn, making
a noise infinitely doleful.

He had a bear-skin to wrap her in, and he
arranged this on the seat beside him and then
tried to wait patiently. He sat very tense and
motionless, except for an occasional glance at his
watch, until it showed exactly seven-thirty.
Then he got out of his car and began walking
first to one side of the corner and then to the
other, for he did not know from which direction
she would come. At twenty-five minutes of eight
he was angry, but in another ten minutes anger
had given way to a dull heavy disappointment
that seemed to hold him by the throat and make

it difficult to swallow. None-the-less he waited a full hour before he started up his car and drove slowly back to the hotel.

On the way he debated with himself whether he should try to communicate with her tonight or wait until the next day. He knew that the wisest thing would be to wait until the next day and send her a note, but he also knew that he could not wait. He would find out where she lived, call her on the telephone, and learn what had prevented her from keeping the appointment. He had desperate need to know that something besides her own will had kept her away.

When he went to the hotel desk, a clerk handed him a letter.

"This was here when you registered, I think," he said. "But I didn't know it. I'm sorry."

When he saw the handwriting of the address he was filled with commotion. Here, then, was her explanation. This would tell him why she had failed him. This, in all probability, would make all right.

He went to his room to read it, sat down on the edge of the bed and ripped the envelope open with an impatient finger. The letter was dated two days earlier—the day after she had received his telegram.

"I don't know what to say," she wrote, "but it doesn't matter much. You will despise me any-

way, and I despise myself. But I can't help it
—honestly I can't. I meant to keep my
promise and I would have kept it, but they found
your telegram and mother read it—by mistake, of course. I ought to have had sense
enough to burn it. You can't imagine how awful
it has been. Mother said the most terrible
things about you, things she had heard. And she
said that I would be ruining my life and hers.
I said I didn't care, because I loved you. I can't
tell you what an awful quarrel we had! And I
wouldn't have given in, but she told Gordon and
he was so terribly angry. He said it was a dis-
grace to the family, and he began to cough and
had a hemorrhage and we thought he was going
to die. Mother said he probably would die unless I gave you up.

"That finished me. I couldn't do anything
after that—I just couldn't. There was nothing
but misery in sight either way, so what was
the use? I've lost all my courage and all my
doubts have come back. I do love you—terribly.
But you are so strange, so different. And
I don't think we would have gotten along or
anything. I try to comfort myself by thinking
it's all for the best, but it doesn't really comfort
me at all. I never knew people could be as
miserable as I am now. I don't think its fair.

"When you get this I will be on my way to

[194]

New York and nearly there. We are going to sail for Europe immediately. I will never see you again. I will always love you.

                                    "Julia."

Rage possessed him at first—the rage of defeated desire, of injured pride, of a passionate, undisciplined nature crossed and beaten. He flung the letter on the floor, and strode up and down the room, looking about for something to smash or tear. So she was that kind of a creature—a miserable, whimpering fool that would let an old woman and a sick man rule her! She was afraid her brother might die. What an excuse! And he had killed, or at least sanctioned killing, for her sake. He had poured out his blood for her. There was nothing he would not have dared or done to have her. And here she had the soul of a sheep!

But no—perhaps that was not it. Perhaps she had been playing with him all along, had never had any idea of marrying him— because he was a Mexican!

Bitter was this thought, but it died as his anger died. Something that sat steady and clear inside of him told him that he was a fool. He was reading the letter again, and he knew it was all truth. "There was nothing but misery in sight either way," she had written.

Suddenly he understood; suffering and an awakened imagination had given him insight. For the first time in his life, he realized the feelings of another. He realized how much he had asked of this girl, who had all her life been ruled, who had never tasted freedom nor practised self-reliance. He saw now that she had rebelled and had fought against the forces and fears that oppress youth, as had he, and that she had been bewildered and overcome.

His anger was gone. All hot emotion was gone. In its place was a great loneliness, tinged with pity. He looked at the letter again. Its handwriting showed signs of disturbance in the writer, but she had not forgotten to scent it with that faint delightful perfume which was forever associated in his mind with her. It summoned the image of her with a vividness he could not bear.

But courage and pride are not killed at a blow. He threw the letter aside and shook himself sharply, like a man just awake trying to shake off the memory of a nightmare. She was gone, she was lost. Well, what of it? There were many other women in the world, many beautiful women. And he was strong now, successful. One woman could not hurt him by her refusal. He tried resolutely to put her out of his mind, and to think of his business, of his plans. But these things which had glowed so brightly in his imagination just a few hours before were suddenly as dead as cinders. He knew that he cared little for dollars and lands in themselves. His nature demanded a romantic object, and this love had given it to him. Love had found him a wretch and a weakling, and had made him suddenly strong and ruthless, bringing out all the colours of his being, dark and bright, making life suddenly intense and purposeful.

And she had meant so much to him besides love. To have won her would have been to win a great victory over the gringos—over that civilization, alien to him in race and temper, which antagonized and yet fascinated him, with which he was forced to grapple for his life.

She was gone, he had lost her. Perhaps it was just as well, after all, he told himself, speaking out of his pride and his courage. But in his heart was a great bitterness. In his heart he felt that the gringos had beaten one more Delcasar.

CHAPTER XXVIII

The next few days Ramon spent quietly and systematically drinking whisky. This he did partly because he had a notion that it was an appropriate thing to do under the circumstances, and partly because he had a genuine need for something to jolt his mind out of its rut of misery. He was not sociable in his cups, and did not seek company of either sex, inviting a man to drink with him or accepting such an invitation only when he had to do so. His favourite resort was the Silver Dollar Saloon, which was furnished with tables set between low partitions, so that when he had one of these booths to himself he enjoyed a considerable degree of isolation. He drank carefully, like a Spaniard, never losing control of his feet or of his eyes, taking always just enough to keep his mind away from realities and filled with dreams. In these dreams Julia played a vivid and delightful part. He imagined himself encountering her under all sorts of circumstances, and always she was yielding, repentant, she was his. In a dozen different ways he conquered her, taking in imagination, as men have always done, what the reality had denied. Some of his fancies were delightful and filled him with a sense of triumph, so that men glanced curiously at the bright-eyed boy who sat there in his corner all alone, absorbed and intent. But there were other times at night when his defeated desire came and lay in his arms like an invisible unyielding succuba, torturing, maddening, driving him back to the street to drink until drunken sleep came with its sudden brutal mercy.

But after a few days alcohol began to have little effect upon him, except that when he awoke his hands were all aflutter so that he spilled his coffee and tore his newspaper. He felt sick and weary, his misery numbed by many repetitions of its every twinge. A sure instinct urged him to get out of the town and into the mountains, but he hated to go alone and lacked the initiative to start. He had a friend in the capital named Curtis, who was half Mexican and half Irish. This young man was a dealer in mules and horses, and he had a herd of some twenty head to take across the mountains about sixty miles. Badly in need of a helper and unable to hire one, he asked Ramon to go with him. The proposition was accepted with relief but without enthusiasm.

Trouble started immediately. The horses were only half broken, and the one they chose for a pack animal rebelled ten miles from town and bucked the pack off, scattering tin dishes, sides of bacon, loaves of bread and cans of condensed milk all over a quarter of a mile of rough country. They rounded up the recalcitrant in a pouring rain, and made a wet and miserable camp, sleeping the sleep of exhaustion in sodden blankets. The next morning the pack horse opened the exercises by rolling down a steep bank into the creek, plastering himself on the way from head to tail with a half gallon of high grade sorghum syrup which had been on top of the load. At this Ramon's tortured nerves exploded and he jumped into the water after the floundering animal, belabouring it with a quirt, and cursing it richly in two languages.

He then put a slip noose around its upper lip and led it unmercifully, while Curtis encouraged it from behind with a rope-end. Like all Mexicans, they had little sympathy for horseflesh.

These labours and hardships were Ramon's salvation. The exercise and air restored his health and in fighting the difficulties of unlucky travel he relieved in some degree the rage against life that embittered him.

When he got back to his room in the hotel he felt measurably at peace, though weary in mind and body. He came across Julia's letter, and the sight and scent of it struck him a sharp painful blow, but he did not pause now to savour his pain; he tore the letter into small pieces and threw it away. Then he got out his car and started for home.

He went back beaten over the same road that he had followed in the moment of his highest hope, when life had seemed about to keep all the wonderful promises it whispers in the ear of youth. But strangely this trip was not the sad and sentimental affair it should have been. His rugged health had largely recovered from the shock of disappointment and dissipation, an excellent breakfast was digesting within him, the sky was bright as polished turquoise and the ozonous west wind, which is the very breath of hope, played sweetly in his face. He began to discover various consoling conditions in his lot, which had seemed so intolerable just a few days before.

Probably no man under forty ever lost a woman without feeling in some degree compensated by a sense of freedom regained, and in the man of solitary and self-reliant nature, to whom freedom is a boon if not a necessity, this feeling is not slow to assert itself. Moreover, Ramon was now caught in the inevitable reaction from a purpose which had gathered and concentrated his energies with passionate intensity for almost four months. During that time he had lived with taut nerves for a single hope; he had turned away from a dozen alluring by-paths; he had known that absorbed

[201]

singleness of purpose which belongs only to lovers, artists and other monomaniacs.

The bright hope that had led him had suddenly exploded, leaving him stunned and flat for a time. Now he got to his feet and looked about. He realized that the world still lay before him, a place of wonderful promise and possibility, and apparently he could stray in any direction he chose. He had money and freedom and an excellent equipment of appetites and curiosities. Things he had dreamed of doing long ago, in case he should ever come into his wealth, now revisited his imagination. He had promised himself for one thing some hunting trips—long ones into the mountains and down the river in his car. Gambling had always fascinated him, and he had longed to sit in a game high enough to be really interesting, instead of the quarter-limit affair that he had always played before. And there were women ... other women. And he meant to go to New York or Chicago sometime and sample the fleshpots of a really great city . . . . Life after all was still an interesting thing.

Not that he forgot his serious purposes. He meant to open a law office, to cultivate his political connections, to pursue his conquest of Arriba County. But although he did not realize it, his plans for making himself a strong and secure position in life had lost their vitalizing purpose. All of these things he would do, but there was no hurry about them. His desire now was to taste the sweetness of life, and to rest. He was without a strong acquisitive impulse, and now that his great purpose in making money was gone, these projects did not strongly engage his imagination. He had plenty of money. He refused to worry. He felt reckless, too. If he had lost his great hope, his reward was to be released from the discipline it had imposed.

Nor was there any other discipline to take its place. If there had been a strong creative impulse in him, or if he had faced a real struggle for his life or his personal freedom, he might now have recovered that condition of trained and focussed energy which civilized life demands of men. But he was too primitive to be engaged by any purely intellectual purpose, and his money was a buffer between him and struggle imposed from without.

As he thought of all the things he would do, he felt strong and sure of himself. He thought that he was now a shrewd, cynical man, who could not be deceived or imposed upon, who could take the good things of life and discount the disillusionments.

CHAPTER XXIX

One of his first acts in town was to negotiate a note at the bank for several thousand dollars. This was necessary because he had little cash and would not have much until spring, when he would sell lambs and shear his sheep. He not only needed money for himself, but his mother and sister, after many lean years, were eager to spend.

He drove out to see Catalina, and found her big with child and utterly indifferent to him, which piqued him slightly and relieved him a great deal. She had heard nothing about her father, and Ramon sent Cortez out to Domingo Canyon to see what had become of the old man. Cortez reported the place deserted. Ramon made inquiry in town and learned that Archulera had been seen there in his absence, very much dressed-up and very drunk, followed by a crowd of young Mexicans who were evidently parasites on his newly-acquired wealth. Then he had disappeared, and some thought he had gone to Denver. It was evident that his five thousand dollars had proved altogether too much for him.

Ramon now hung out a shingle, announcing himself as an attorney-at-law. Of course, no business came to him. The right way to get a practice would have been to go back to the office of Green or some other established lawyer for several years. But Ramon had no idea of doing anything so tiresome and so relatively humiliating. The idea of running errands for Green again was repugnant to him.

He went every morning to his office and for a while he took a certain amount of satisfaction in merely sitting there, reading the local papers, smoking a cigar, now and then taking down one of his text books and reading a little. But study as such had absolutely no appeal to him. He might have dug at the dry case books to good purpose if he had been driven by need, but as it was he would begin to yawn in ten or fifteen minutes, and then would put the book away. He went home to a noonday dinner rather early and came back in the afternoon, feeling sleepy and bored. Now the office, and indeed the whole town, seemed a dreary place to him. At this season of the year there were often high winds which mantled the town in a yellow cloud of sand, and rattled at every loose shutter and door with futile dreary persistence. Ramon would wander about the office for a little while with his hands in his pockets and stare out the window, feeling depressed, thoughts of his disappointment coming back to him bitterly. Then he would take his hat and go out and look for some one to play pool with him. Often he took an afternoon off and went hunting, not alone as formerly he had done, but with as large a party as he could gather. They would drive out into the sand hills and *mesas* twenty or thirty miles from town, where the native quail and rabbits were still abundant as automobiles had just begun to invade their haunts. When they found a covey of quail the sport would be fast and furious, with half a dozen guns going at once and birds rising and falling in all directions. Ramon keenly enjoyed the hot excitement and dramatic quality of this.

At night he was usually to be found at the White Camel Pool Hall where the local sporting element foregathered and made its plans for the evening. Sometimes a party would be formed to "go down the line," as a visit to the red light district was called. Sometimes the rowdy dance halls of Old Town were invaded. On Saturday nights the dance at the country club always drew a considerable attendance. There was also a "dancing class" conducted by an estimable and needy spinster named Grimes, who held assembly dances once in two weeks in a little hall which had been built by the Woman's Club. This event always drew a large and very mixed crowd, including some of the "best people" and others who were considered not so good. Usually two or three different sets were represented at these gatherings, each tending to keep to itself. But there was also a tendency for the sets to overlap. Thus a couple of very pretty German girls, who were the daughters of a local saloon keeper, always appeared accompanied by young men of their own circle with whom they danced almost exclusively at first. But young men of the first families could not resist their charms, and they soon were among the most popular girls on the floor. This was deplored by the young women of more secure social position, who were wont to remark that the crowd was deteriorating frightfully. Some of these same superior virgins found it necessary for politeness to dance with Joe Bartello, the son of an Italian saloon owner, and a very handsome and nimble-footed youth. In a word, this was a place of social hazard and adventure, and that was more than half its charm. It finally became so crowded that dancing was almost impossible.

The back room at the White Camel, where poker games were nightly in progress, also afforded Ramon frequent diversion. He played in the "big" game now, where the stakes and limits were high, and was one of the most daring and dangerous of its patrons. He had more money back of him than most of the men who played there, and he also had more courage. If he started a bluff he carried it through to the end, which was always bitter for some one. He had been known to stand pat on a pair and scare every one else out of the game by the resolute confidence of his betting. His plunges, of course, sometimes cost him heavily, but for a long time he was a moderate winner. His limitations as a poker player were finally demonstrated to him by one Fitzhugh Chesterman, a man with one lung.

Chesterman was about twenty-six years old and had come from Richmond, Virginia, about two years before, with most of one lung gone and the other rapidly going. He was a tall, thin blond youth with the sensitive, handsome face which so often marks the rare survivor of the old southern aristocracy. He was totally lacking in the traditional southern sentimentality. His eye had a cold twinkle of courage that even the imminent prospect of death could not quench, and his thin shapely lips nearly always wore a smile slightly twisted by irony. He established himself at the state university, which had almost a hundred students and boasted a dormitory where living was very cheap. Chesterman sat before this dormitory twelve to fourteen hours a day, even in relatively cold weather. He made a living by coaching students in mathematics and Greek. He never raised his voice, he seldom laughed, he never lost his temper. With his unwavering ironical smile, as though he appreciated the keen humour of taking so much trouble over such an insignificant thing as a human life, he husbanded his energy and fought for health. He took all the treatments the local sanatoria afforded, but he avoided carefully all the colonies and other gatherings of the tubercular. When his lung began to heal, as it did after about a year, and his strength to increase, he enlarged his earnings by playing poker. He won for the simple reason that he took no more chances than he had to. He systematically capitalized every bit of recklessness, stupidity and desperation in his opponents.

When Ramon first encountered him, the game soon simmered down to a struggle between the two. Never were the qualities of two races more strikingly contrasted. Ramon bluffed and plunged. Chesterman was caution itself, playing out antes in niggardly fashion until he had a hand which put the law of probabilities strongly on his side. Ramon was full of daring, intuition, imagination, bidding always for the favour of the fates, throwing logic to the winds. He was not above moving his seat or putting on his hat to change his luck. Chesterman smiled at these things. He was cold courage battling for a purpose and praying to no deities but Cause and Effect. Ramon thought he was playing for money, but he was really playing for the sake of his own emotions, revelling alike in hope and despair, triumph and victory, flushed and bright-eyed. Chesterman stifled every emotion, discounted every hope, said as little as possible, never relaxed his faint twisted smile.

Ramon made some spectacular winnings, but Chesterman wore him down as surely as a slow hound wears down a deer despite its astounding bursts of speed. Ramon was sure to lose in the long run because he was always piling up odds against himself by the long chances he took, while his bluffs seldom deceived his cool and courageous opponent. The finish came at one o'clock in the morning. Chesterman was pale with exhaustion, but otherwise unchanged. Ramon was hoarse and flushed, chewing a cigar to bits. He held a full house and determined to back it to the limit. Chesterman met him, bet for bet, raising every time. Ramon knew that he must be beaten. He knew that Chesterman would not raise him unless he had a very strong hand. But he was beaten anyway. At the bottom of his consciousness, he knew that he had met a better man. He wanted to end the contest on this hand. When Chesterman showed four kings, Ramon fell back in his chair, weak and disgusted. The other players, most of whom had long been out of the game, got up and said good night one by one. Only the two were left, Ramon plunged in gloomy reaction, Chesterman coolly counting his money, putting it away.

"I seem to have made quite a killing," he remarked, "how much did you lose?"

"O, I don't know . . . about five hundred. Hell, what's five hundred to me . . . . I don't give a damn . . . I'm rich. . . ."

Chesterman glanced at him keenly.

"Well," he remarked, "I'm glad you feel that way about it, because I sure need the money."

He got up and walked away with the short careful steps of a man who cherishes every ounce of his energy.

Ramon was disgusted with himself. Chesterman had made him feel like a weakling and a child. He had thought himself a lion in this game, and he had found out that he was an easily-shorn lamb. He could not afford to lose five hundred dollars either. He was not really a rich man. He went home feeling deeply depressed and discouraged. Vaguely he realized that in Chesterman he had encountered the spirit which he felt against him everywhere—a cool, calculating, unmerciful spirit of single purpose, against which the play and flow of his emotional and imaginative nature was as ineffectual as mercury against the point of a knife.

CHAPTER XXX

Within the next few days Ramon was sharply reminded that he lived in a little town where news travels fast and nobody's business is exclusively his own. Cortez came into his office and accepted a seat and a cigar with that respectful but worried manner which always indicated that he had something to say.

"I hear you lost five hundred dollars the other night," he observed gravely, watching his young employer's face.

"Well, what of it?" Ramon enquired, a bit testily.

"You can't afford it," Cortez replied. "And not only the money . . . you've got to think of your reputation. You know how these gringos are. They keep things quiet. They expect a young man to lead a quiet life and tend to business. It's all right to have a little fun . . . they all do it . . . but for God's sake be careful. You hurt your chances this way . . . in the law, in politics."

Ramon jerked his head impatiently and flushed a little, but reflection checked his irritation. Hatred of restraint, love of personal liberty, the animal courage that scorns to calculate consequences were his by heritage. But he knew that Cortez spoke the truth.

"All right Antonio," he said with dignity. "I'll be careful."

The next day he got a letter which emphasized the value of his henchman's warning and made Ramon really thoughtful. It was from Mac-Dougall, and made him another offer for his land. It had a preamble to the effect that land values were falling, money was "tight," and therefore Ramon would do well to sell now, before a further drop in prices. It made him an offer of ten thousand dollars less than MacDougall had offered before.

Ramon knew that the talk about falling values was largely bluff, that MacDougall had heard of his losses and of his loose and idle life, and thought that he could now buy the lands at his own price. The gringo had confidently waited for the Mexican to make a fool of himself. Ramon resolved hotly that he would do no such thing. He had no idea of selling. He would be more careful with his money, and next summer he would go back to Arriba County, renew his campaign against MacDougall and buy some land with the money he could get for timber and wool. He replied very curtly to MacDougall that his lands were not for sale.

After that he stayed away from poker games for a while. This was made easier by a new interest which had entered his life in the person of a waitress at the Eldorado Lunch room. The girls at this lunch room had long borne a bad reputation. Even in the days before the big hotel had been built, when the railroad company maintained merely a little red frame building there, known as the Eating House, these waitresses had been a mainstay of local bachelordom. Their successors were still referred to by their natural enemies, the respectable ladies of the town, as "those awful eating house girls"; while the advent of a new "hash-slinger" was always a matter of considerable interest among the unmarried exquisites who fore-gathered at the White Camel. In this way Ramon quickly heard of the new waitress. She was reputed to be both prettier and less approachable than most of her kind. Sidney Felberg had made a preliminary reconnaissance and a pessimistic report.

"Nothing doing," he said. "She's got a husband somewhere and a notion she's cut out for better things. . . . I'm off her!"

This immediately provoked Ramon's interest. He went to the lunch room at a time when he knew there would be few customers. When he saw the girl he felt a faint thrill. The reason for this was that Dora McArdle somewhat resembled

Julia. The resemblance was slight and superficial, yet instantly noticeable. She was a little larger, but had about the same figure, and the same colour of hair, and above all the same sensuous, provocative mouth. Ramon followed her with his eyes until she became conscious of his scrutiny, when she tossed her head with that elaborate affectation of queenly scorn, which seems to be the special talent of waitresses everywhere. Nevertheless, when she came to take his order she gave him a pleasant smile. He saw now that she was not really like Julia. She was coarse and commonplace, but she was also shapely, ripe-breasted, good-natured, full of the appeal of a healthy animalism.

"What time do you get done here?" Ramon enquired.

"Don't know that it's any of your business," she replied with another one of her crushing tosses of the head, and went away to get his order. When she came back he asked again.

"What time did you say?"

"Well, about nine o'clock, if it'll give you any pleasure to know."

"I'll come for you in my car," he told her.

"Oh! will you?" and she paid no more attention to him until he started to go, when she gave him a broad smile, showing a couple of gold teeth.

At nine o'clock he was waiting for her at the

[215]

door, and she went with him. He took her for a drive on the *mesa*, heading for the only road house which the vicinity boasted. It was a great stone house, which had been built long ago by a rich man, and had later fallen into the hands of an Italian named Salvini, who installed a bar, and had both private dining rooms and bed rooms, these latter available only to patrons in whom he had the utmost confidence. This resort was informally known as the "chicken ranch."

When Ramon tried to take his fair partner there, on the plea that they must have a bite to eat, she objected.

"I don't believe that place is respectable," she told him very primly. "I don't think you ought to ask me to go there."

"O Hell!" said Ramon to himself. But aloud he proposed that they should drive to an adjacent hill-top from which the lights of the town could be seen. When he had parked the car on this vantage point and lit a cigarette, Dora began a narrative of a kind with which he was thoroughly familiar. She was of that well-known type of woman who is found in a dubious position, but explains that she has known better days. Her father had been a judge in Kansas, the family had been wealthy, she had never known what work was until she got married, her marriage had been a tragedy, her husband had drank, there had been a

smash-up, the family had met with reverses. On
and on went the story, its very tone and character
and the grammar she used testifying eloquently to
the fact that she was no such crushed violet as
she claimed to be. Ramon was bored. A year
ago he would have been more tolerant, but now he
had experienced feminine charm of a really high
order, and all the vulgarity and hypocrisy of this
woman was apparent to him. And yet as he sat
beside her he was keenly, almost morbidly conscious of the physical attraction of her fine young
body. For all her commonness and coarseness,
he wanted her with a peculiarly urgent desire.
Here was the heat of love without the flame and
light, desire with no more exaltation than ac-
companies a good appetite for dinner. He was
puzzled and a little disgusted.... He did not
understand that this was his defeated love, seeking, as such a love almost inevitably does, a vicari-
ous satisfaction.

Repugnance and desire struggled strangely
within him. He was half-minded to take her
home and leave her alone. At any rate he was
not going to sit there and listen to her insane babble all night. To put his fortunes to the test, he
abruptly took her in his arms. She made a futile
pretence of resistance. When their lips touched,
desire flashed up in him strongly, banishing all his
hesitations. He talked hot foolishness to which

she listened greedily, but when he tried to take her to Salvini's again, she insisted on going home. Before he left her he had made another appointment.

Now began an absurd contest between the two in which Ramon was always manœuvring to get her alone somewhere so that he might complete his conquest if possible, while her sole object was to have him gratify her vanity by appearing in public with her. This he knew he could not afford to do. He could not even drive down the street with her in daylight without all gossips being soon aware he had done so. No one knew much about her, of course, but she was "one of those eating house girls" and to treat her as a social equal was to court social ostracism. He would win the enmity of the respectable women of the town, and he knew very well that respectable women rule their husbands. His prospects in business and politics, already suffering, would be further damaged.

Here again was a struggle within him. He was of a breed that follows instinct without fear, that has little capacity for enduring restraints. And he knew well that the other young lawyers, the gringos, were no more moral than he. But they were careful. Night was their friend and they were banded together in a league of obscene secrecy. He despised this code and yet he feared it. For the gringos held the whip; he must either cringe or suffer.

So he was careful and made compromises. Dora wanted him to take her to dinner in the main dining room of the hotel, and he evaded and compromised by taking her there late at night when not many people were present. She wanted him to take her to a movie and he pleaded that he had already seen the bill, and asked her if she wanted to bore him. And when she pouted he made her a present of a pair of silk stockings. She accepted all sorts of presents, so that he felt he was making progress. She was making vague promises now of "sometime" and "maybe," and his desire was whipped up with anticipation, making him always more reckless.

One night late he took her to the Eldorado and persuaded her to drink champagne, thinking this would forward his purpose. The wine made her rosy and pretty, and it also made her forget her poses and affectations. She was more charming to him than ever before, partly because of the change in her, and partly because his own critical faculties were blunted by alcohol. He was almost in love with her and he felt sure that he was about to win her. But presently she began wheedling him in the old vein. She wanted him to take her to the dance at the Woman's Club!

This would be to slap convention in the face,

and at first he refused to consider it. But he foolishly went on drinking, and the more he drank the more feasible the thing appeared. Dora had quit drinking and was pleading with him.

"I dare you!" she told him. "You're afraid ...You don't think I'm good enough for you... And yet you say you love me . . . I'm just as good as any girl in this town . . . Well if you won't, I'm going home. I'm through! I thought you really cared."

And then, when he had persuaded her not to run away, she became sad and just a little tearful.

"It's terrible," she confided. "Just because I have to make my own living... Its not fair. I ought never to speak to you again...And yet, I do care for you. . . ."

Ramon was touched. The pathos of her situation appealed strongly to his tipsy consciousness. Why not do it? After all, the girl was respectable. As she said, nobody "had anything on her." The dance was a public affair. Any one could go. He had been too timid. Not three people there knew who she was. By God, he would do it!

At first they did not attract much attention. Dora was pretty and fairly well dressed, in no way conspicuous. They danced exclusively with each other, as did some other couples present, and nothing was thought of that.

But soon he became aware of glances, hostile, disapproving. Probably it was true that only a few of the men at first knew who Dora was, but they told other men, and some of the men told the women. Soon it was known to all that he had brought "one of those awful eating house girls" to the dance! The enormity of the mistake he had made was borne in upon him gradually. Some of the men he knew smiled at him, generally with an eye-brow raised, or with a shake of the head. Sidney Felberg, who was a real friend, took him aside.

"For the love of God, Ramon, what did you bring that Flusey here for? You're queering yourself at a mile a minute. And you're drunk, too. For Heaven's sake, cart her away while the going's good!"

Ramon had not realized how drunk he was until he heard this warning.

"O, go to hell, Sid!" he countered. "She's as good as anybody . . . I guess I can bring anybody I want here. . . ."

Sidney shook his head.

"No use, no use," he observed philosophically. "But it's too bad!"

Ramon's own words sounded hollow to him. He was in that peculiar condition when a man knows that he is making an ass of himself, and knows that he is going right ahead doing it. He

was more attentive to Dora than ever. He
brought her a glass of water, talked to her continually with his back to the hostile room. He was
fully capable of carrying the thing through, even
though girls he had known all his life were refusing to meet his eyes.

It was Dora who weakened. She became
quiet and sad, and looked infinitely forlorn.
When a couple of women got up and moved
pointedly away from her vicinity, her lip began
to tremble, and her wide blue eyes were brimming.

"Come on, take me away quick," she said path-
etically. "I'm going to cry."

When they were in the car again she turned in
the seat, buried her face in her arms and sobbed
passionately with a gulping noise and spasmodic
upheavals of her shoulders. Ramon drove
slowly. He was sober now, painfully sober!
He was utterly disgusted with himself, and bitterly sorry for Dora. A strong bond of sympathy had suddenly been created between them,
for he too had tasted the bitterness of prejudice.
For the first time Dora was not merely a frumpy
woman who had provoked in him a desire he half-
despised; she was a fellow human, who knew the
same miseries. . . . He had intended to take her
this night, to make a great play for success, but
he no longer felt that way. He drove to the
boarding house where she lived.

"Here you are," he said gently, "I'll call you up tomorrow."

Dora looked up for the first time.

"O, no!" she plead. "Don't go off and leave me now. Don't leave me alone. Take me somewhere, anywhere. . . . Do anything you want with me. . . . You're all I've got!"

CHAPTER XXXI

The rest of the winter Ramon spent in an aimlessly pleasant way. He tried to work but without arousing in himself enough enthusiasm to insure success. He played pool, gambled a little and hunted a great deal. He relished his pleasures with the keen appetite of health and youth, but when they were over he felt empty-minded and restless and did not know what to do about it.

Some business came to his law office. Because of his knowledge of Spanish and of the country he was several times employed to look up titles to land, and this line of work he might have developed into a good practice had he possessed the patience. But it was monotonous, tedious work, and it bored him. He would toil over the papers with a good will for a while, and then a state of apathy would come over him, and like a boy in school he would sit vaguely dreaming. . . . Such dull tasks took no hold upon his mind.

He defended several Mexican criminals, and found this a more congenial form of practice, but an unremunerative one. The only case which advanced him toward the reputation for which every young attorney strives brought him no money at all. A young Mexican farmer of good reputation named Juan Valera had been converted to the Methodist faith. Like most of the few Mexicans who are won over to Protestantism, he had brought to his new religion a fanatical spirit, and had made enemies of the priests and of many of his neighbours by proselyting. Furthermore, his young and pretty wife remained a Catholic, which had caused a good deal of trouble in his house. But the couple were really devoted and managed to compromise their differences until a child was born. Then arose the question as to whether it should be baptized a Catholic or a Methodist. The girl wanted her baby to be baptized in the Catholic faith, and was fully persuaded by the priests that it would otherwise go to purgatory. She was backed by her father, whose interference was resented by Juan more than anything else. He consulted the pastor of his church, a bigoted New Englander, who counselled him on no account to yield.

One evening when Juan was away from home, his father-in-law came to his house and persuaded the girl to go with him and have the child baptized in the Catholic faith, in order that it might be saved from damnation. After the ceremony they went to a picture-show by way of a celebration. When Juan came home he learned from the neighbours what had happened. His face became very pale, his lips set, and his eyes had a hot, dangerous look. He got out a butcher knife from the kitchen, whetted it to a good point, and went and hid behind a big cottonwood tree near the moving-picture theatre. When his wife with the child and her father came out, he stepped up behind the old man and drove the knife into the back of his neck to the hilt, severing the spinal column. Afterward he looked at the dead man for a moment and at his wife, sitting on the ground shrieking, then went home and washed his hands and changed his shirt—for blood had spurted all over him—walked to the police station and gave himself up.

This man had no money, and it is customary in such cases for the court to appoint a lawyer to conduct the defence. Usually a young lawyer who needs a chance to show his abilities is chosen, and the honor now fell upon Ramon.

This was the first time since he had begun to study law that he had been really interested. He understood just how Juan Valera had felt. He called on him in jail. Juan Valera was composed, almost apathetic. He said he was willing to die, that he did not fear death.

"Let them hang me," he said. "I would do the same thing again."

Ramon studied the law of his case with exhaustive thoroughness, but the law did not hold out much hope for his client. It was in his plea to the jury that he made his best effort. Here again he discovered the eloquence that he had used the summer before in Arriba County. Here he lost for a moment his sense of aimlessness, felt again the thrill of power and the joy of struggle. He described vividly the poor Mexican's simple faith, his absolute devotion to it, showed that he had killed out of an all-compelling sense of right and duty. He found a good many witnesses to testify that Juan's father-in-law had hectored the young man a good deal, insulted him, intruded in his home. Half of the jurors were Mexicans. For a while the jury was hung. But it finally brought in a verdict of murder in the first degree, which was practically inevitable. Juan accepted this with a shrug of his shoulders and announced himself ready to hang and meet his Methodist God. But Ramon insisted on taking an appeal. He finally got the sentence commuted to life imprisonment. He then felt disgusted, and wished that he had let the man hang, feeling that he would have been better off dead than in the state penitentiary. But Juan's wife, who really loved him, came to Ramon's office and embraced his knees and laughed and cried and swore that she would do his washing for nothing as long as she lived. For now she could visit her husband once a month and take him *tortillas!* Ramon

[227]

gave her ten dollars and pushed her out the door. He had worked hard on the case. He felt old and weary and wanted to get drunk.

One day Ramon received an invitation to go hunting with Joe Cassi and his friends. He accepted it, and afterward went on many trips with the Italian saloon-owner, thereby doing further injury to his social standing.

Cassi had come to the town some twenty years before with a hand organ and a monkey. The town was not accustomed to that form of entertainment; some of the Mexicans threw rocks at Cassi and a dog killed his monkey. Cassi was at that time a slender youth, handsome, ragged and full of high hopes. When his monkey was killed he first wept with rage and then swore that he would stay in that town and have the best of it. He now owned three saloons and the largest business building in town. He was a lean, grave, silent little man.

Cassi had made most of his money in the days when gambling was "open" in the town, and he had surrounded himself with a band of choice spirits who were experts in keno, roulette and poker. These still remained on his hands, some of them in the capacity of barkeepers, and others practically as pensioners. They were all great sportsmen, heavy drinkers and loyal-to-the-death friends. At short intervals they went on hunting trips down the river, generally remaining over the week-end. It was of these expeditions that Ramon now became a regular member. Sometimes the whole party would get drunk and come back whooping and singing as the automobiles bowled along, occasionally firing shotguns into the air. At other times when luck was good everyone became interested in the sport and forgot to drink. Ramon had a real respect for Cassi, and a certain amount of contempt for most of the rest of them; yet he felt more at home with these easy-going, pleasure-loving, loyal fellows than he did with those thrifty, respectable citizens in whose esteem the dollar stood so invariably first.

Cassi and his friends used most often to go to a Mexican village some fifty miles down the river where the valley was low and flat, and speckled with shallow alkaline ponds made by seepage from the river. Every evening the wild ducks flew into these ponds from the river to feed, and the shooting at this evening flight Ramon especially loved. The party would scatter out, each man choosing his own place on the East side of one of the little lakes, so that the red glare of the sunset was opposite him. There he would lie flat on the ground, perhaps making a low blind of weeds or rushes.

Seldom even in January was it cold enough to

be uncomfortable. Ramon would lie on an elbow, smoking a cigarette, watching the light fade, and the lagoon before him turn into molten gold to match the sunset sky. It would be very quiet save for such sounds as the faraway barking of dogs or the lowing of cattle. When the sky overhead had faded to an obscure purple, and the flare of the sunset had narrowed to a belt along the horizon, he would hear the distant eerie whistle of wild wings. Nothing could be seen yet, but the sound multiplied. He could distinguish now the roar of a great flock of mallards, circling round and round high overhead, scouting for danger. He could hear the sweet flute-notes of teal and pintails, and the raucous, cautious quack of some old green-head. A teal would pitch suddenly down to the water before him and rest there, erect and wary, painted in black upon the golden water. Another would join it and another. The cautious mallards, encouraged by this, would swing lower. The music of their wings seemed incredibly close; he would grip his gun hard, holding himself rigidly still, feeling clearly each beat of his heart.

Suddenly the ducks would come into view . . . dark forms with ghostly blurs for wings, shooting with a roar into the red flare of light. The flash of his shotgun would leap out twice. The startled birds would bound into the air like blasted rock from a quarry, and be lost in the purple mystery of sky, except two or three that hurtled over and over and struck the water, each with a loud spat, throwing up little jets of gold.

Sometimes there were long waits between shots, but at others the flight was almost continuous, the air seemed full of darting birds, and the gun barrels were hot in his hands. His excitement would be intense for a time; yet after he had killed a dozen birds or so he would often lose interest and lie on his back listening to the music of wings and of bird voices. He had that aversion to excess which seems to be in all Latin peoples. Besides, he did not want many ducks to dispose of. . . . It was the rush and colour, the dramatic quality of the thing that he loved.

Most of the others killed to the limit with a fine unflagging lust for blood, giving a brilliant demonstration of the fact that civilized man is the most destructive and bloodthirsty of all the predatory mammals.

The coming of spring was marked by a few heavy rains, followed by the faint greening of the cottonwood trees and of the alfalfa fields. The grey waste of the *mesa* showed a greenish tinge, too, heralding its brief springtime splendor when it would be rich with the purple of wild-peas, pricked out in the morning with white blossoms of the prairie primrose. Now and then a great flock of geese went over the town, following the Rio Grande northward half a mile high, their faint wild call seeming the very voice of this season of lust and wandering.

Ramon felt restless and lost interest in all his usual occupations. He began to make plans and preparations for going to the mountains. He bought a tent and a new rifle and overhauled all his camping gear. He thought he was getting ready for a season of hard work, but in reality his strongest motive was the springtime longing for the road and the out-of-doors. He was sick of whisky and women and hot rooms full of tobacco smoke.

Withal it was necessary that he should go to Arriba County, follow up his campaign of the preceding fall, arrange a timber sale if possible so that he might buy land, and above all see that his sheep herds were properly tended. This was the crucial season in the sheep business. Like the other sheep owners, he ranged his herds chiefly over the public domain, and he gambled on the weather. If the rain continued into the early summer so that the waterholes were filled and the grass was abundant, he would have a good lamb crop. The sale of part of this and of the wool he would shear would make up the bulk of his income for the year. And he had already spent that income and a little more. He could not afford a bad year. If it was a dry spring, so that lambs and ewes died, he would be seriously embarrassed. In any case, he was determined to be on the range in person and not to trust the herders. If it came to the worst and the spring was dry he would rent mountain range from the Forest Service and rush his herds to the upland pastures as early as possible. He was not at all distressed or worried; he knew what he was about and had an appetite for the work.

One morning when he was in the midst of his preparations, he went to his office and found on the desk a small square letter addressed in a round, upright, hand. This letter affected him as though it had been some blossom that filled the room with a fragrant narcotic exhalation. It quickened the beat of his heart like a drug. It drove thought of everything else out of his mind. He opened it and the faint perfume of it flowed over him and possessed his senses and his imagination. . . .

It was a long, gossipy letter and told him of nearly everything that Julia had done in the six months since they had parted "forever". The salient fact was that she had been married. A young man in a New York brokerage office who had long been a suitor for her hand, and to whom she had once before been engaged for part of a summer, had followed the Roths to Europe and he and Julia had been married immediately after their return.

"I give you my word, I don't know why I did it," she wrote. "Mother wanted me to, and I just sort of drifted into it. First thing I knew I was engaged and the next thing mother was sending the invitations out, and then I was in for it. It was a good deal of fun being engaged, but when it came to being married I was scared to death and couldn't lift my voice above a whisper. Since then it has been rather a bore. Now my husband has been called to London. I am living alone here in this hotel. That is, more or less alone. A frightful lot of people come around and bore me, and I have to go out a good deal. I'm supposed to be looking for an apartment, too; but I haven't really started yet. Ralph won't be back for another two or three weeks, so I have plenty of time.

"I don't know why in the world I'm writing you this long frightfully intimate letter. I don't seem to know why I do anything these days. I know its most improper for a respectable married lady, and I certainly have no reason to suppose you want to be bothered by me any more after the way I did. But somehow you stick in the back of my head. You might write me a line, just out of compassion, if you're not too busy with all your sheep and mountains and things." She signed herself "as ever", which, he reflected bitterly, might mean anything.

At first the fact that she was married wholly engaged his attention. She was then finally and forever beyond his reach. This was the end sure enough. He was not going to start any long aimless correspondence with her to keep alive the memory of his disappointment. He planned various brief and chilly notes of congratulation. . . . Then another thought took precedence over that one. She was alone there in that hotel. Her husband was in London. She had written to him and given him her address. . . . His blood pounded and his breath came quick. He made his decision instantly, on impulse. He would go to New York.

He wired the hotel where she was stopping for a reservation, but sent no word at all to her. He gave the bewildered and troubled Cortez brief orders by telephone to go to Arriba County in his place, arranged a note at the bank for two thousand dollars, and caught the limited the same night at seven-thirty-five.

CHAPTER XXXII

He looked at New York through a taxicab window without much interest. A large damp grey dirty place, very crowded, where he would not like to live, he thought. He managed himself and his baggage with ease and dispatch; his indifferent, dignified manner and his reckless use of money were ideally effective with porters, taxi drivers and the like. When he reached the hotel about eight o'clock at night he went to his room and made himself carefully immaculate. He studied himself with a good deal of interest in the full length mirror which was set in the bath room door; for he had seldom encountered such a mirror and he had a considerable amount of vanity of which he was not at all conscious. It struck him that he was remarkably good-looking, and indeed he was more so than usual, his eyes bright, his face flushed, his whole body tense and poised with purpose and expectation.

He went down to the lobby, looked Julia up in the register, ascertained the number of her room, and made a note of it. Then he asked the telephone girl to call her and learn whether she was in.

[236]

"Yes; she is in. She wants to know who's calling, please."

"Tell her an old friend who wants to surprise her." He did not care to risk any evasion, and he also wanted his arrival to have its full dramatic effect.

The telephone girl transmitted his message.

"She says she can't come down yet . . . not for about half an hour."

"Tell her I'll wait. If she asks for me I'll be in that little room there." He pointed to a small reception room opening off the mezzanine gallery, which he had selected in advance. He had planned everything carefully.

When he stood up to meet her she gave a little gasp, and took a step back.

"Why, you! Ramon! How could you? You shouldn't have come. You know you shouldn't. I didn't mean that . . . I had no idea. . . ."

He came forward and took her hand and led her to a settee. Despite all her protests he could see very plainly that he had scored heavily in his own favour. She was flustered with excitement and pleasure. Like all women, she was captivated by sudden, decisive action and loved the surprising and the dramatic.

They sat side by side, looking at each other,

smiling, making unimportant remarks, and then looking at each other again. Ramon felt that she had changed. She was as pretty as ever, and never had she stirred him more strongly. But her appeal seemed more immediate than before; she seemed less remote. The innocence of her wide eyes was a little less noticeable and their flash of recklessness a little more so. It seemed to him that her mouth was larger, which may have been due to the fact that she had rouged it a little too much. She wore a pink decollete with straps over the shoulders one of which kept slipping down and had to be pulled up again.

Ramon was tremulous with a half-acknowledged anticipation, but he held himself strongly in hand. He felt that he had an advantage over her— that he was more at ease and she less so than at any previous meeting—and he meant to keep it.

But she was rapidly regaining her composure, and took refuge in a rather formal manner.

"Are you going to be here long?" she enquired in the conventional tone of mock-interest.

"Just a week or so on business," he explained, determined not to be outpointed in the game. "I had to come some time this spring, and when I got your note I thought I would come while you are here."

"But I'll be here the rest of my life probably. This is where I live. You ought to have come

when my husband was here. I'd like to have you
meet him. As it is, I can't see much of you, of
course. . . ."

He refused to be put out by this coldness, but
tried to strike a more intimate note.

"Tell me about your marriage," he asked.
"Are you really happy? . . . Do you like it?"

She looked at the floor gravely.

"You shouldn't ask that, of course," she re-
proved. "Everyone who has just been married
is very, very happy. . . . No, I don't like it a
darn bit."

"It's not what you expected, then."

"I don't know what I expected, but from the
way people talk about it and write about it you
would certainly think it was something wonderful
—love and passion and bliss and all that, I mean.
I feel that I've either been lied to or cheated . . .
of course" she added with a little side glance at
him, "I didn't exactly love my husband. . . ."
She blushed and looked down again; then laughed
softly and rather joyfully for a lady with a broken
heart.

"If mother could only hear me now!" she
observed. . . . "She'd faint. I don't care. . . .
That's just the way I feel. . . . I don't care!
All my life I've been trained and groomed and
prepared for the grand and glorious event of
marriage. I've been taught it's the most wonder-

ful thing that can happen to anyone. That's what all the books say, and all the people I know. And here it turns out to be a most uncomfortable bore. . . ."

He looked gravely sympathetic.

"Do you think it would have been different with—someone you did love?" he enquired cautiously.

She gave him another quick thrilling glance.

"I don't know," she said. . . . "Maybe. . . . I felt so different about you."

Their hands met on the settee and they both moved instinctively a little closer together.

Suddenly she jerked away from him, looking him in the eyes with her head thrown back and a smile of irony on her lips.

"Aren't we a couple of idiots?" she demanded.

"No!" he declared with fierce emphasis, and throwing an arm about her, pounced on her lips.

Just then a bell boy passed the door. They jerked apart and upright very self-consciously. Then they looked at each other and laughed. But their eyes quickly became deep and serious again, and their fingers entangled.

She sighed in mock exasperation.

For Heaven's sake, say something!" she demanded. "We can't sit here and make eyes at each other all evening. Besides I'm compromising my priceless reputation. It's after ten o'clock.

I've got to go." She rose, and held out her hand, which he took without saying anything.

"Good night," she said. "I think you were mean to come and camp on me this way . . . dumb as ever, I see . . . well, good night."

She went to the door, stopped and looked back. smiled and disappeared.

Ramon went down to the lobby and roamed all over the two floors which constituted the public part of the hotel. He looked at everything and smoked a great many cigarettes, thus restlessly whiling away an hour. Then he went to a writing room. He collected some telegrams and letters about him and appeared to be very busy. When a bell boy went by, he rapped sharply on the desk with a fifty-cent piece, and as the boy stopped, tossed it to him.

"Get me the key to 207!" he ordered sharply; then turned back to his imaginary business.

"Yes sir." said the boy. He returned in a few minutes with the key.

Ramon sat for a long moment looking at it, tremulous with a great anticipation. He was divided between a conviction that she expected him and a fear that she did not. . . . His fear proved groundless.

CHAPTER XXXIII

The next day they met for dinner at a little place near Washington Square where it was certain that none of Julia's friends ever went. Julia was a singularly contented-looking criminal. Never, Ramon thought had her skin looked more velvety, her eyes deeper or more serene. He was a trifle haggard, but happy, and both of them were hungry.

"Do you know? . . . I've made a discovery," she told him. "I haven't any conscience. I slept peacefully nearly all day, and when I waked up I considered the matter carefully . . . I don't believe that I have any proper appreciation of the enormity of what I've done at all. I have always thought that if anything like this ever happened to me I would go off and chloroform myself, but as a matter of fact I have no such intention . . . of course, though, it was not my fault in the least. You're so terrible! . . . I simply couldn't help myself, and I don't see what I can do now . . . that's comforting. But one thing is certain. We've got to be awfully careful. Thank Heaven, mother and Gordon are still in Florida and they won't dare to come North on Gordon's account until it gets a good deal warmer. But we must be careful. I'm not sorry, like I should be, but I sure am scared. . . ."

They sat for a long time after the meal, Ramon smoking a cigar, their knees touching under the table. He was filled with a vast contentment. He thought nothing of the troubled past, nor did he look into the obviously troubled future. He merely basked in the consciousness of a possession infinitely sweet.

Now began for them a life of clandestine adventure. Julia had a good many engagements, but she managed to give him some part of every day. They never met in the hotel, but usually took taxicabs separately and met in out-of-the-way parts of that great free wilderness of city. Ramon spent most of the time when he was not with her exploring for suitable meeting places. They became patrons of cellar restaurants in Greenwich Village, of French and Italian places far down town, of obscure Brooklyn hotels. If the regular fare at these establishments was not all they desired, Ramon would lavishly bribe the head waiter, call the proprietor into consultation if necessary, insist on getting what Julia wanted. He spent his money like a millionaire, and usually created the general impression that he was a wealthy foreigner. Every morning he had flowers sent to Julia's room. Often they would take a taxi and spend hours riding about the streets with the blinds drawn, locked in each others' arms.

For a week they were keenly, excitedly happy, living wholly in the joy of the moment. Then a flaw appeared upon the glowing perfect surface of their happiness.

"When is your husband coming back?" he enquired once, when they were riding through Central Park.

"I don't know. In a week or two. Why?"

"Because we must decide pretty soon what we're going to do."

"Do? What can we do?"

"We must decide where we're going. You must go with me somewhere. I'm not going to let you get away from me again . . . not even for a little while."

"But Ramon, how can we? I'm married. I can't go anywhere with you. . . ."

He seized her fiercely by the shoulders and held her away from him, looking into her eyes.

"Don't you love me, then?" he demanded.

"Ramon! You know I do!"

"Then you'll go. We can go to Mexico City, or South America . . . I'll sell out at home. . . ."

"O, Ramon . . . I can't. I haven't got the courage. Think of the fuss it would raise. And it would kill Gordon, I know it would. . . ."

"Damn Gordon!" he exclaimed, "he's not going to get in the way again! You're mine and I'm going to keep you. You will go. I'll take you!"

He had seized her in his arms, was holding her furiously tight. She put her arms around him, caressed his face with soft fluttering hands.

"Please, Ramon! Please don't make me miserable. Don't spoil the only happiness I ever had! I will go with you if ever I can, if I can get a divorce or something. But I can't run off like that. I haven't got it in me . . . please let me be happy!"

Her touch and her voice seemed to overcome his determination, seemed to sheer him of his strength. Weaker she was than he, but her charm was her power. It dragged him away from his thoughts and purposes, binding him to her and to the moment. . . . She drew his head down to her breast, found his lips with hers and so effectively cut his protests short.

The cream of his happiness was gone. Always when he was alone, he was thinking and planning how he could keep her. All of his possessiveness was aroused. He wanted her to have a baby. Somehow he felt that then his conquest would be complete, that then he would be at peace. . . .

He said nothing more to Julia because he saw

that it was useless. He began to understand her a little. It was futile to ask her to make a decision, to take any initiative. She could hold out forever against pleas which involved an effort of the will on her part. And yet as he knew she could yield charmingly to pressure adroitly applied. If he had asked her to meet him in New York this way, he reflected, she would have been horrified, she would never have consented. But when he came, suddenly, that had been different. So it was now. If he could only form a really good plan, and then put her in a cab and take her . . . that would be the only way. The difficulty was to form the plan. He had capacity for sudden and decisive action. He lacked neither courage nor resolution. But when it came to making a plan which would require much time and patience, he found his limitations.

What could he do? he asked himself, not realizing that in formulating the question he acknowledged his impotence. If he went away and left her while he settled his affairs, she was lost as surely as a bird released from a cage. The idea of Mexico City allured him. But he had hardly enough money to take them there. How could he raise money on short notice? It would take time to settle his estate in New Mexico and get anything out of it. . . .

Two unrealized facts lay at the root of his

difficulty. One was that he had no capacity for large and intricate plans, and the other was that he felt bound as by an invisible tether to the land where he had been born.

As he struggled with all these conflicting considerations and emotions, his head fairly ached with futile effort. He was glad to lay it upon Julia's soft bosom, to forget everything else again in the sweetness of a stolen moment.

CHAPTER XXXIV

He had been in New York about ten days when he awoke one morning near noon. An immense languor possessed him. He had been with Julia the night before and never had she been more charming, more abandoned. . . . He ordered his breakfast to be sent up, and then stretched out in bed and lit an expensive Russian cigarette. He had that love of sensuous indolence, which, together with its usual complement, the capacity for brief but violent action, marked him as a primitive man—one whom the regular labors and restraints of civilization would never fit.

His telephone bell rang, and when he took down the receiver he heard Julia's voice. It was not unusual for her to call him about this time, but what she told him now caused a blank and hapless look to come over his face. She was not in her room, but in another hotel.

"My husband got in this morning," she explained in a voice that was thin with misery and confusion. "I got his message last night, but I didn't tell you because I knew it would spoil our last time together, and I was afraid you would do something foolish. . . . Please say you're not angry. You know there was nothing for it. We couldn't have done any of those wild things you talked about. I'll always love you, honestly I will. Won't you even say goodby? . . ."

He at last did say goodby and hung up the receiver and went across the room and sat in an armchair. It suddenly struck him that he was very tired. He had not realized it before . . . how tired he was. There was none of the mad rebellion in him now that had filled him when first she had run away from him. Although he had never acknowledged it to himself he had been more than half prepared for this. He had told himself that he was going to do something bold and decisive, but he had procrastinated; he had never really formed a plan.

Weariness was his leading emotion. He was spent, physically and emotionally. He wanted her almost as much as ever. While she was no longer the remote and dazzling star she had been, the bond of flesh that had been created between them seemed a stronger, a more constant thing than blinding unsatisfied desire. But a great despair possessed him. There was so obviously nothing he could do. Just as his other disappointment had given him his first stinging impression of the irony of life, that cunningly builds a hope and then smashes it; so now he felt for the first time something of the helplessness of man in the

[249]

current of his destiny, driven by deep-laid desires
he seldom understands, and ruled by chances he
can never calculate. From love a man learns
life in quick and painful flashes.

Through the open window came the din of the
New York street—purr and throb of innumerable
engines, rumble and clatter of iron wheels, tapping
of thousands of restless feet, making a blended
current of sound upon which floated and tossed the
shrillness of police whistles and newsboys' voices
and auto horns. It had been the background of
his life during memorable days. Once it had
stirred his pulses, seeming a wild accompaniment
to the song of his passion. Now it wearied him
inexpressibly; it seemed to be hammering in his
ears; he wanted to get away from it. He would
go home that day.

As always on his trips across the continent he
sat apathetically smoking through the wide green
lushness of the middle west. Only when the
cultivated lands gave way to barren hills and
faint blue mountains peeping over far horizons
did he turn to the window and forget his misery
and his weariness. How it spoke to his heart,
this country of his own! He who loved no man,
who had gone to women with desire and come
away with bitterness, loved a vast and barren
land, baking in the sun. The sight of it quickened

his pulses, softened and soothed his spirit. Like a good liquor it nursed and beautified whatever mood was in him. When he had come back to it a year before, it had spoken to him of hope, its mysterious distances had seemed full of promise and hidden possibility. And now that he came back to it with hopes broken, weary in mind and body, it seemed the very voice of rest. He thought of long cool nights in the mountains and of the lullaby that wind and water sing, of the soothing monotony of empty sunlit levels, of the cool caress of deep, green pools, of the sweet satisfaction that goes with physical weariness and a full belly and a bed upon the ground.

But when on the last morning of his journey he waked up within a hundred miles of home, and less than half that far from his own mountain lands, his new-found comfort quickly changed to a keen anxiety. For he saw at a glance that the country was under the blight of drought. The hills that should have borne a good crop of gramma grass at this time of the year, if the rains had been even fair, were nothing but bare red earth from which the rocks and the great roots of the *pinion* trees stood out like the bones of a starving animal. Here and there on the hillsides he could see a scrubby pine that had died, its needles turned rust-red—the sure sign of a serious drought.

During the half month that he had been gone he had thought not once of his affairs at home. The moment had absorbed him completely. Now it all came back to him suddenly. When he had left, the promise of the season had been good. It had not rained for more than a week, but everyone had been expecting rain every day. It was clear to him that the needed rain had never come. And he knew just what that meant to him. It meant that he had lost lambs and ewes, that he would have no money this year with which to meet his notes at the bank. He sank deep in despair and disgust again. Not only was the assault on his fortunes a serious one, but he felt little inclined to meet it. He was weary of struggle. He saw before him a long slow fight to get on his feet again, with the chance of ultimate failure if he had another bad year.

The Mexicans firmly believe, in the face of much evidence to the contrary, that seven wet years are always followed by seven dry ones. He had heard the saying gravely repeated many times. He more than half believed it. And he knew that for a good many years, perhaps as many as six or seven, the rains had been remarkably good. He was intelligent, but superstition was bred in his bones. Like all men of a primitive type he had a strong tendency to believe in fortune as a deliberate force in the affairs of men. It seemed clear to him now, in his depressed and exhausted condition, that bad luck had marked him for its prey.

CHAPTER XXXV

His forebodings were confirmed in detail the next morning when Cortez came into his office, his face wrinkled with worry and darkened by exposure to the weather. He was angry too.

"*Por Dios,* man! To go off like that and not even leave me an address. If I could have gotten more money to hire men I might have saved some of them . . . yes, more than half of the lambs died, and many of the ewes. There is nothing to do now. They are on the best of the range, and it has begun to rain in the mountains. But it is too bad. It cost you many thousands . . . that trip to New York."

Ramon gave Cortez a cigar to soothe his sensibilities, thanked him with dignity for his loyal services, and sent him away. Then he put on his hat and went outside to walk and think.

The town seemed to him quiet as though half-deserted. This was partly by contrast with the place of din which he had just left, and partly because this was the dull season, when the first hot spell of summer drove many away from the town and kept those who remained in their houses most of the day. The sandy streets caught the sun and cherished it in a merciless glare. They were baked so hot that barefoot urchins hopped gingerly from one patch of shade to the next. In the numerous vacant lots rank jungles of weeds languished in the dry heat, and long blue-tailed lizards, veritable heat-sprites, emerged to frolic and doze on deserted sidewalks. The leaves of the cottonwoods hung limp, and the white downy tufts that carried their seeds everywhere drifted and swam in the shimmering air. The river had shrunk to a string of shallow pools in a sandy plain, the irrigation ditches were empty, and in Old Town the Mexicans were asking God for rain by carrying an image of the Virgin Mary about on a litter and firing muskets into the air.

Quickly wearied, Ramon sat down on a shaded bench in the park and tried to think out his situation and to decide what he should do. The easy way was to sell out, pay his debts, provide for his mother and sister and with what was left go his own way—buy a little ranch perhaps in the mountains or in the valley where he could live in peace and do as he pleased. Wearied as he was by struggle and disappointment, this prospect allured him, and yet he could not quite accept it. He felt vaguely the fact that in selling his lands, he would be selling out to fate, he would be surrendering to MacDougall, to the gringos, he would be renouncing all his high hopes and dreams.

[255]

His mountain lands, with their steadily increasing value, the power they gave him, would make of his life a thing of possibilities—an adventure. Settled on a little ranch somewhere, his whole story would be told in one of its years.

This he did not reason clearly, but the emotional struggle within him was therefore all the stronger. It was his old struggle in another guise—the struggle between the primitive being in him and the civilized, between earth and the world of men. Each of them in turn filled his mind with images and emotions, and he was impotent to judge between them.

His being was fairly rooted in the soil, and the animal happiness it offered—the free play of instinct, the sweetness of being physically and emotionally at peace with environment—was the only happiness he had ever known. Vaguely yet surely he had felt the world of men and works, the artificial world, to contain something larger and more beautiful than this. Julia Roth had been to him a stimulating symbol of this higher, this more desirable thing. His love for her had been the soil in which his aspirations had grown. That love had turned to bitterness and lust, and his aspirations had led him among greeds and fears and struggles that differed from those of the wild things only in that they were covert and devious, lacking the free beauty of instinct fearlessly followed and the dignity of open battle. Of civilization he had encountered only the raw and ugly edge, which is uglier than savagery. He knew no more of the true spirit of it than a man who has camped in a farmer's back pasture knows of the true spirit of wildness. It had treated him without mercy and brought out the worst of him. And yet because he had once loved and dreamed he could not go back to the easy but limited satisfactions of the soil and be wholly content.

So he could not make up his mind at first to surrender, but in the next few days one thing after another came to tempt him that way. MacDougall made him an offer for his lands which to his surprise was a little better than the last one. He learned afterward that the over-shrewd lawyer had misinterpreted his trip to New York, imagining that he had gone there to interest eastern capital in his lands.

His mother and sister were two very cogent arguments in favour of selling. The Dona Delcasar, a simple and vain old lady, now regarded herself as a woman of wealth, and was always after him for money. Her ambition was to build a house in the Highlands and serve tea at four o'clock (although it was thick chocolate she liked) and break into society. His one discussion of the matter with her was a bitter experience.

"Holy Mary!" she exclaimed in her shrill Spanish, when he broached a plan of retrenchment, "What a son I have! You spend thousands on yourself, chasing women and buying automobiles, and now you want us to spend the rest of our lives in this old house and walk to church so that you can make it up. God, but men are selfish!"

He saw that if he tried to save money and make a fight for his lands he would have to struggle not only with MacDougall and the weather, but with two ignorant, ambitious and sharp-tongued women. And family pride here fought against him. He did not want to see his women folk go shabbily in the town. He wanted them to have their brick house and their tea parties, and to uphold the name of Delcasar as well as they might.

One day while he was still struggling with his problem he went to look at a ranch that was offered for sale in the valley a few miles north of town. It was this place more than anything else which decided him. The old house had been built by one of his ancestors almost a hundred years before, and had then been the seat of an estate which embraced all the valley and *mesa* lands for miles in every direction. It had changed hands several times and there were now but a few hundred acres. The woodwork of the house was in bad repair, but its adobe walls, three feet thick, were firm as ever. There were still traces of the adobe stockade behind it, with walls ten feet high, and the building which had housed the *peones* was still standing, now filled with fragrant hay. In front of it stood an old cedar post with rusty iron rings to which the recalcitrant field hands had been bound for beating.

Every detail of this home of his forefathers stirred his emotions. The ancient cottonwood trees in front of the house with their deep, welcome shade and the soft voices of courting doves among the leaves; the alfalfa fields heavy with purple blossom, ripe for cutting; the orchard of old apple trees and thickets of Indian plum run wild; the neglected vineyard that could be made to yield several barrels of red wine—all of these things spoke to him with subtle voices. To trade his heritage for this was to trade hope and hazard for monotonous ease; but with the smell of the yielding earth in his nostrils, he no more thought of this than a man in love thinks of the long restraints and irks of marriage when the kiss of his woman is on his lips.

CHAPTER XXXVI

Ramon's life on his farm quickly fell into a routine that was for the most part pleasant. He hired an old woman to do his cooking and washing, and a man to work on the place. Other men he hired as he needed them, and he spent most of his days working with them as a foreman.

He attended to the business of farming ably. The trees of the old orchard he pruned and sprayed and he set out new ones. He put his idle land under irrigation and planted it in corn and alfalfa. He set out beds of strawberries and asparagus. He bought blooded livestock and chickens. He put his fences in repair and painted the woodwork of his house. The creative energy that was in him had at last found an outlet which was congenial though somewhat picayune. For the place was small and easily handled. As the fall came on, and his crops had been gathered and the work of irrigation was over for the season, he found himself looking about restlessly for something to do. On Saturday nights he generally went to town, had dinner with his mother and sister, and spent the evening drinking beer and playing pool. But he felt increasingly out of place in the town; his visits there were prompted more by filial duty and the need of something to break the monotony of his week than by a real sense of pleasure in them.

He was still caring for Catalina on the ranch up the valley, and when the woman who had been doing his work left him, he decided to bring the girl to his place and let her earn her keep by cooking and washing. He no longer felt any interest in her, and thought that perhaps she would marry Juan Cardenas, the man who milked his cows and chopped wood for him. But Catalina showed no interest in Juan. Instead, she emphatically rejected all his advances, and displayed an abject, squaw-like devotion to Ramon's welfare. Everything possible was done for his comfort without his asking. The infant, now almost a year old, was trained not to cry in his presence, and acquired a certain awe of him, watching him with large solemn eyes whenever he was about. Ramon, reflecting that this was his son, set out to make the baby's acquaintance, and became quite fond of it. He often played with it in the evening.

He paid Catalina regular wages and she spent most of the money on clothes. When she prepared herself for Church on Sunday she was a truly terrible spectacle, clad in an ill-fitting ready-made suit of brilliant colour, and wearing a cheap hat on which a dead parrot sprawled among artificial poppies, while her swarthy face, heavily powdered, took on a purple tinge. But about the place, dressed in clean calico, with a shawl over her shoulders, she was really pretty. Her figure was a good one of peasant type, and the acquisition of some shoes which fitted her revealed the fact that she had inherited from her remote Castilian ancestry a small and shapely foot and ankle.

Ramon could not help noticing all of these things, and so gradually he became aware of Catalina again as a desirable woman, and one whom it was easy for him to take.

After this his animal contentment was deeper than ever. He did not go to town so often, for one of the restlessnesses which had driven him there was removed. Often for weeks at a stretch he would not go at all unless it was necessary to get some tools or supplies for the farm. Then rather than take any of his men away from work, he would himself hitch up a team and drive the five miles. Sitting hunched over on the spring-seat of a big farm wagon, clad in overalls and a print shirt, with a wide hat tilted against the sun and a cigarette dangling from his lips, he was indistinguishable from any other *paisano* on the road. This change in appearance was helped by the fact that he had grown a heavy moustache. Often, as he drove through the streets of the town, he would pass acquaintances who did not recognize him, and he was just as well satisfied that they did not.

As is the way of unreflecting men, Ramon formed no definite opinion of his life, but liked it more or less according to the mood that was in him. There were bright, cool days that fall when, lacking work to do, he took his shot-gun and a saddle horse and went for long rambles. Sometimes he would follow the river northward, stalking the flocks of teal and mallards that dozed on the sandbars in the wide, muddy stream, perhaps killing three or four fat birds. Other times he went to the foot of the mountains and hunted the blue quail and cotton tail rabbits in the arroyos of the foot-hills. Once he and his man loaded a wagon with food and blankets and drove forty miles to a canyon where they killed a big black-tail buck, and brought him back in high triumph.

Returning from such trips full of healthy hunger and weariness, to find his hot supper and his woman waiting for him, Ramon would doze off happily, every want of his physical being satisfied, feeling that life was good. . . . But there were other nights when a strange restlessness possessed him, when he lay miserably awake through long dark hours. The silence of the black valley was emphasized now and then by the doleful voices of dogs that answered each other across the sleeping miles. At such times he felt as though he had been caught in a trap. He saw in imagination the endless unvaried chain of his days stretching before him, and he rebelled against it and knew not how to break it. His experience of life was comparatively little and he was no philosopher. He did not know definitely either what was the matter with him or what he wanted. But he had tasted high aspiration, and desire bright and transforming, and wild sweet joy. . . . These things had been taken away, and now life narrowed steadily before him like a blind canyon that pierces a mountain range. The trail at the bottom was easy enough to follow, but the walls drew ever closer and became more impassable, and what was the end? . . .

This sense of dissatisfaction reached its futile crux one day in the spring when he received a letter from Julia—the last he was ever to get. The sight and scent of it stirred him as they always had done, filling him with poignant painful memories.

"This is really the last time I'll ever bother you," she wrote, "but I do want to know what has happened to you, and how you feel about things.

I can't forget. All our troubles seem to have worn some sort of a permanent groove in my poor brain, and I believe the thought of you will be there till the day of my death.

"As for me, I'm in society up to my eyes, and absolutely without the courage or energy to climb out. Those days in New York were the first and the last of my freedom. Now I've been introduced to everybody, and I have an engagement book that tells me what I'm going to do whether I want to or not for three weeks ahead. I'm a model of conduct and propriety for the simple reason that I can't travel over a block without everybody that I know finding out about it.

"Of course it hasn't all been a bore. I have had some fun, and I've met some really interesting people. I've gotten used to being married and my husband treats me kindly and gives me a good home. Sounds as if I was a kitten, doesn't it? Well, I have very much the same sort of life as a kitten, but a kitten has no imagination and it has never been in love. Sometimes I think that I can't stand it any longer. It seems to me that I'm not really living, as I used to imagine I would, but just being dragged through life by circumstances and other people—I don't know what all. I still have desperate plans and ideas once in a while, but of course, I never do anything. When you come right down to it, what can I do?"

[265]

Ramon read this letter sitting on the sunny side of his house with his heels under him and his back against the wall—a position any Mexican can hold for hours. When he had finished it he sat motionless for a long time, painfully going over the past, trying ineptly to discover what had been the matter with it. More acutely than ever before he felt the cruel guerdon of youth—the contrast between the promise of life and its fulfillment. He felt that he ought to do something, that he ought not to submit. But somehow all the doors that led out of his present narrow way into wider fields seemed closed. There was no longer any entrancing vista to tempt him. Mentally he repeated her query, What could he do?

His thoughts went round and round and got nowhere. The spring sunshine soaked into his body. A faint hum of early insects lulled him, and to his nostrils came the scent of new-turned earth and manure from the garden where his man was working. He grew drowsy; his dissatisfaction simmered down to a vague ache in the background of his consciousness. Idly he tore the letter to little bits.

THE END